PUFFIN BOOKS

RAGS AND RICHES

Sam and her brother, Seb, live with their flamboyant mother, Isabella, in a narrow street in Edinburgh. Across the road, in a basement, is the second-hand clothes shop which Isabella runs, not very profitably. They have a continuing struggle to survive financially — their father, Torquil, who comes and goes (like driftwood, as their granny says), is of little help. They would not manage to survive at all if it were not for their grandmother. She is not the kind of granny who sits in the chimney corner shrouded in shawls; she tints her hair auburn, manages a local supermarket, and goes for trips to places like Tenerife. And when the cat's away . . . But when she's at home, Granny is a formidable lady who sees her main role in life as that of trying to keep Isabella's 'batty' family on the rails.

The ups-and-downs of the family are related in turn by Sam and Seb, through whom we meet their friends Morag (nice name, Morag, says Granny, who thinks Sam and Seb sound like a couple of cartoon characters) and Hari, whose family lead a 'normal' life; Torquil's father who lives in a crumbling and mist-bound castle in Argyll, and Torquil's sister Clementina who is known as the giddy aunt and whose three rumbustious small daughters, Daisy, Buttercup and Clover, are nicknamed the Flowers of the Field.

This is a highly entertaining and humorous book.

Joan Lingard lives in Edinburgh where she was born, though she was brought up in Belfast. She is the author of nineteen novels for young people and eleven for adults. She likes travelling and visits North America every year with her Canadian husband. She has three daughters.

Rags and Riches

by
Joan Lingard

PUFFIN BOOKS

PUFFIN BOOKS

Published by the Penguin Group
27 Wrights Lane, London W8 5TZ, England
Viking Penguin Inc., 40 West 23rd Street, New York, New York 10010, USA
Penguin Books Australia Ltd, Ringwood, Victoria, Australia
Penguin Books Canada Ltd, 2801 John Street, Markham, Ontario, Canada L3R 1B4
Penguin Books (NZ) Ltd, 182–190 Wairau Road, Auckland 10, New Zealand

Penguin Books Ltd, Registered Offices: Harmondsworth, Middlesex, England

First published by Hamish Hamilton Children's Books 1988
Published in Puffin Books 1990
1 3 5 7 9 10 8 6 4 2

Printed and bound in Great Britain by
Richard Clay Ltd, Bungay, Suffolk
Filmset in Palatino

For Sally Floyer
and for
Lucy, Biddy, Toby and Hugo

Contents

1

Silver Linings

Sam

Every cloud is supposed to have one, or so I learned at my granny's knee. Isn't that where you're supposed to learn such things? My granny is full of sayings, most of them rubbish, according to my mother, who has plenty of her own. Like most mothers. My granny isn't one of those grandmothers who sits and knits in the chimney corner, shrouded in shawls, if such grannies exist at all. She tints her hair auburn and is employed as manageress at a local supermarket. It's not all that 'super', I must add, as it's only got two aisles, one up and one down, but still, a job's a job these days. And money doesn't grow....

Money's a problem in our family and my granny helps keep us afloat with 'care' parcels. She dumps them down on the kitchen table muttering about the improvidence of my parents and the wasted education of my mother who had all the chances in life that she didn't have herself. Etcetera. My father is not a lot of use when it comes to providing. He does odd jobs and he comes and goes. Like driftwood, says my granny, who doesn't understand what her daughter saw in him.

I think it was probably his name. He's called Torquil. My mother's got a thing about names. Her own given name was Isabel. A good plain no-nonsense Scottish name. The only person who uses it now is my granny. My mother is known to everyone else as Isabella or Bella.

My name is Samantha, which my mother uses in full, but my friends call me Sam and my brother's called Seb, short for Sebastian. My granny approves of neither the short nor the long versions. 'Sam and Seb — sounds like two cartoon characters!' She hates having to introduce us, it gives her a 'red face'. She had wanted us to be called Jean and Colin. So she calls me hen (that's a Scottish endearment, for those who don't know) and Seb, son.

Anyway, to get back to silver linings. I don't know about clouds having them but for a short time we had in our possession a fur coat which had one. But, first, I'd better explain about my mother's shop.

She keeps a second-hand clothes shop in a street that's full of shops selling second-hand things, from books to old fenders and clocks to medals and feather boas (though they're scarce) and silk petticoats (usually full of snags and runs) and woollens (usually matted). There are also two or three bars in the street, and some cafés. We like it, Seb and I. There's always something going on. The shop's in a basement (a damp one) across the road from our flat. You can doubtless imagine what my granny thinks of it. She says the smell of the old clothes turns her stomach and folk that buy stuff like that need their heads examined.

But people do come in and buy, not that it's ever like the shops in Princes Street on a Saturday. And they tend to sit on boxes and blether to my mother for hours before they get round to buying some ghastly looking dress with a V neck and a drooping hemline that was fashionable during the war. And then they find they

2

haven't got quite enough money to pay for it so she says she'll get it from them the next time they're in. You can see why we need the care parcels.

When my mother goes out on the rummage for our new stock — new old stock, that is — she just shuts up the shop and leaves a note on the door saying 'Back in ten minutes' or, if I'm home from school, she leaves me in charge with my friend Morag. (Nice name, Morag, says my granny.) Morag and I amuse ourselves by trying on the clothes and parading up and down like models. We usually have a good laugh, too. I like long traily dresses in black crêpe de Chine and big floppy hats, and Morag likes silks and satins. We don't bother with the matted woollies.

One day my mother came back in a taxi filled to bursting with old clothes. She was bursting with excitement too, even gave the taxi driver a pound tip. You'd have thought we were about to make our fortune!

Morag and I helped to haul in the catch. We sat on the floor in the middle of it and unpacked the bags. There were dresses of every colour of the rainbow, made of silk and of satin, of brocade and of very fine wool.

'They belonged to an old lady,' said my mother.

The dresses smelt really old when you pressed them to your face.

'She died last month.'

We shivered a little and let the dresses fall into our laps.

'She was *very* old, though.'

We cheered up and turned our attention to the blouses and scarves and the satin shoes. The old lady must never have thrown anything away.

And then out of a bag I took a fur coat. Now my mother doesn't like fur coats, usually won't handle them.

By that, I mean sell them. She's for Beauty Without Cruelty. As I am myself. But this coat felt kind of smooth and silky, even though it was a bit bald looking here and there, and so I slipped it on.

'I'll have to get rid of that quickly,' said my mother.

I stroked the fur.

'Poor animal,' said my mother.

I slipped my hands into the pockets. I was beginning to think there was something funny about the coat. The lining felt odd, sort of lumpy, and I thought I could hear a faint rustling noise coming from inside it. I took the coat off.

The lining had been mended in a number of places by someone who could sew very fine stitches. I lifted the scissors and quickly began to snip the thread.

'What are you doing that for?' asked my mother irritably.

'Wait!'

I eased my hand up between the lining and the inside of the coat and brought out a five pound note. Morag gasped. And then I brought out another and another and then a ten pound one and then another five and a ten—

'I don't believe it!' said my mother, who looked as pale as the off-white blouse she was crumpling between her hands.

We extracted from the lining of the coat one thousand and ten pounds in old bank notes. They were creased and aged, but they were real enough. We sat in silence and stared at them. My mother picked up a ten pound note and peered at it in the waning afternoon light.

'She can't have trusted the bank. Old people are sometimes funny that way. Keep their money in mattresses and places.'

Like old coats.

'We could go for a holiday,' I said

'A Greek island,' murmured my mother. 'Paros. Or Naxos.'

Once upon a time she used to wander around islands with my father, before Seb and I were born. I could see us, the three of us, lying on the warm sand, listening to the soft swish of the blue, blue sea.

'Are you going to keep it?' asked Morag, breaking into our trance. She's a bit like that, Morag — down-to-earth, a state of being that my granny is fully in favour of.

My mother bit the side of her lip, the way she does when she's confused. She quite often bites her lip.

'Finder's keepers,' I said hopefully. Hadn't my granny taught me that?

'I did *pay* for the coat.'

Not a thousand pounds of course, we knew that.

'Who did you buy it from?' asked Morag.

'A relative of the old lady's. He was clearing out the house. He looked well enough heeled.'

'In that case—' I said.

'I'll need to think about it,' said my mother. 'In the meantime—' She glanced about her and I got up to put on the light and draw the curtains.

What *were* we to do with the money?

'We could sew it back into the coat,' I suggested.

That seemed as good an idea as any other so Morag and I pushed the notes back into the lining, all but one ten pound one which my mother said we might as well keep out to buy something for supper with that evening.

'Morag,' she said, sounding a bit awkward, 'don't be saying anything about this to anyone else, eh?'

'I wouldn't dream of it, Isabella.' (My mother likes my

friends to call her by her Christian name. She likes Seb and me to do it, too, but when I'm talking about her I usually refer to her as 'my mother'.)

When I chummed Morag along the street on her way home I told her I'd kill her if she did tell and we almost quarrelled as she said I'd no business to doubt her word. But it was such a big secret to keep! I felt choked up with the excitement of it.

We took the fur coat across the road when we went home, and over an Indian carry-out and a bottle of rosé wine my mother and Seb and I discussed the problem of whether we were entitled to keep the money or not. Seb and I thought there was no problem at all.

'You bought the coat, Bella,' said Seb. 'Everything in it's yours.'

'Well, I don't know. Maybe legally, but morally ... I mean, I suppose I *should* give it back.'

'But you want to go to Greece, don't you?' I said.

Her lip trembled.

Outside, it was raining. Big heavy drops were striking the window pane and the wind was making the glass rattle in its frame.

'You could both be doing with new shoes,' said our mother. 'Mind you, with money like that. . . .' She sighed.

The next day was Saturday. We took the coat back over to the shop with us in the morning, afraid to let it out of our sight. My mother put it in a cupboard in the back room where she keeps garments that are waiting to be mended. Some are beyond redemption but they wait nevertheless.

In the afternoon, we had to go to a family wedding, on my father's side. My father was supposed to be there. My mother and I kitted ourselves out with clothes from the shop.

'Well, honestly!' declared my granny, on her arrival. She was to mind the shop while we were gone. 'I could have lent you a nice wee suit, Isabel.' She turned to look me over. 'Do you think black crêpe de Chine's the right thing to be wearing at a wedding? And at your age, too!' She didn't even call me hen. She couldn't have thought I looked endearing. The dress had come out of the old lady's wardrobe.

In the bus, Seb said to our mother, 'Now don't tell Father about the money if he *is* there.'

He did turn up. He was his usual 'charming' self, never stuck for words. I was pleased enough to see him to begin with but after a bit when I saw him sweet-talking our mother and her cheeks beginning to turn pink and her eyes lighting up, I felt myself going off him. Seb and I sat side by side and drank as much fizzy wine as we could get hold of and listened to her laugh floating down the room.

'She'll tell him,' said Seb gloomily.

She did, of course. And he decided to come home with her. They walked in front of us, holding hands.

'When will she ever learn?' said Seb, sounding strangely like our granny.

'Good evening, Torquil,' said that lady very stiffly, when we came into the shop where she was sitting playing Clock Patience on the counter top. 'Stranger,' she couldn't resist adding.

'Hi, Ma!' He gave her a smacking kiss on the cheek. 'It's good to see you. You're not looking a day older.'

She did not return the compliment.

'Been busy?' asked my mother.

'Not exactly rushed off my feet. I sold two or three dresses and one of those tatty Victorian nightgowns —

oh, and yon moth-eaten fur coat in the cupboard through the back.'

She might just as well have struck us all down with a sledgehammer. We were in a state of total collapse for at least five minues until my mother managed to get back the use of her tongue.

'You sold *that coat*?'

'Well, why not? You hate having fur lying around.'

'Who did you sell it to?' My mother was doing her best to stay calm.

'How should I know? Some woman. She came in asking if we'd any furs. She gave me twenty pounds for it. I didn't think you could ask a penny more. Lucky to get that.'

My mother told my granny about the money in the lining and then it was her turn to collapse. I thought we were going to have to call a doctor to revive her. My father managed it with some brandy that he had in his coat pocket.

'Oh no,' she moaned, 'oh *no*. But what did you leave it in the shop for, Isabel?'

'It was in the back shop! In the cupboard.'

They started to argue, to blame one another. Seb and I went out and roamed the streets till dark and long after, looking for the woman in our fur coat. We never did see it again.

Our father left the next morning.

'Shows him up for what he is, doesn't it?' said our granny. 'He only came back for the money. He'd have taken you to the cleaners, Isabel. Maybe it was just as well. As I always say——' She stopped.

Not even she had the nerve to look my mother in the eye and say that every cloud has its silver lining.

2

A Head for Figures

Seb

I'm Seb. That's short for·Sebastian. But you know that already, from my sister, Sam. Not that you can take every single thing she says for Gospel (as our grandmother would say), but in this case you can.

Granny took to her bed after the fur coat affair. She was sick 'to her stomach'. It was Sunday so the supermarket was closed. By Monday morning, though, she had recovered her appetite sufficiently to demolish a bowlful of porridge, a kipper, two slices of toast and marmalade and five cups of tea. Strong tea. No messing about with any of that herbal stuff our mother drinks, when she's not drinking strong black coffee, that is. She's not consistent, our mother. But you may have gathered that. Granny itemised her breakfast for us when she called in on her way past to work.

'It would do you both good to eat some decent food in the mornings,' she said, rounding on Sam and me, 'instead of yon muck. Uncooked oats and stuff!'

'Muesli's good for them,' said our mother, who was drinking a cup of coffee and not eating at all, which is the usual way she starts the day. She spoke automatically. She was also in her dressing gown, another habit our grandmother disapproves of. She herself washes and dresses as soon as she rises, before a bite is permitted to cross her lips. She has her standards and we are never allowed to forget what they are.

'Look at the two of you!' said Granny. 'No wonder the country is going to the dogs.'

We pulled ourselves up out of our slumps before she could start on about the benefits of a spell in the army. 'They should bring back conscription. It would make men of you.' This can be guaranteed to start a real rave-up of an argument, with Bella, Sam and me ranged on one side. We have anti-nuclear posters pinned up on the shop walls and when Granny is minding the shop she takes them down. She says the government knows what is best for us. She makes us seethe! I didn't feel like an argument that morning. We'd had enough over the fur coat. I finished off my Physics homework.

'You should have had that done last night, son. And you shouldn't be eating and doing your lessons at the same time. I don't know, Isabel! You weren't brought up like that. I always kept you up to the mark.'

Our mother didn't bother to reply. She had other things on her mind. The usual. Money, of course. The electricity bill had come in the morning post, a reminder, the last one, covered with awful warnings in red. Pay up or else.... Our mother had just had time to push it under a bundle of silk scarves lying on the kitchen table before her mother arrived. Granny has her own key so she can walk in unannounced and catch us in various acts.

Sam scraped back her chair and got up, yawning her head off.

'And what time did you get to your bed last night, young lady?'

'Can't remember. Come on and I'll chum you down the road, Gran. I'm ready for off.'

'You're never going to school in *that*?' Granny stared at the garment in which Sam was got up. It was in the 'forties' style, so I had been informed, and it hung rather oddly on Sam, kind of squint-like, and the shoulders made her look like an American football player. (I'd had to duck when I'd informed *her* of that.)

Sam put on her innocent look. 'Why not, Gran?'

'I don't know what things are coming to, I'm sure. I mind when children used to go to school looking neat and tidy and wearing uniforms.'

'Well, we don't have to wear uniforms now,' said Sam, picking up a pink satin jacket and slinging it over her shoulders.

'Uniforms leave no room for individuals to express their personalities,' said our mother.

Granny trumpeted.

'Come on,' said Sam and took her arm.

They went off. My mother poured herself another cup of coffee and retrieved the electricity bill from beneath the scarves. She examined it again and sighed.

'I don't know where we're going to get the money from. There's the telephone bill, too, and the amount owing to Mr McWhitty for the broken window in the shop....'

And no doubt other odd bits and pieces due to this shopkeeper and that.

'How much do we owe altogether, Bella?'

'I've no idea.' She ran her fingers through her hair. It's of the colour that is sometimes described as 'flaming' red and is something Sam and I have inherited from her. An inheritance from her father's side of the family. Carrot tops, Granny calls us and says she can see us coming a mile off, which is not always to our advantage. 'It's all over there,' said my mother.

11

Over there meant behind the clock that no longer works. It's French ormolu, according to my father, who vows it's worth a fortune, but when he did try to hawk it around the numerous antique shops in the neighbourhood he returned still carrying it and declaring that they didn't know a good thing even when it was shoved under their noses.

I collected the bills and brought them over to the table.

'You count it up, Sebastian. You've got a good head for figures. I'm no use at that kind of thing.'

'You could be if you wanted to. But you don't, do you?'

She was looking at the Articles for Sale in the *Scotsman*. I did a quick count.

'Two hundred and fifty-nine pounds and five pence.'

'Heavens! Where's that going to be found? I've got nine pounds to my name.'

'You could make your customers pay when they buy something.'

'I do! But sometimes they don't have it on them.'

It's not easy having a mother like mine. I tell my friend Hari that but I don't know if he believes me. He thinks she's terribly amusing. He says his own mother is very serious. She's a nurse at the Infirmary. His father's a structural engineer so they both bring home regular salaries and their bills are always paid on time.

'Bella, you've got to learn to be tougher. No money, no deal.'

'I'm sure you'd make a fine business man, Sebastian.'

'Rubbish!' I have plans to be an astronomer. I want nothing to do with selling or with old junk of any kind. 'But if you're going to be in business you'll have to be more business-like.'

12

'You'll be late for school if you don't hurry.'

I put the bills back behind the clock.

'We'll talk about it later,' I said.

'Good idea.'

It was three days before I got her back to the topic. Either her friends were in, or Granny.

'You can't just let this ride, Bella,' I said, when I had a chance to get a word in. 'We'll get the electricity cut off, for one thing. And then we'd have to pay to get connected up again.'

'I intend to pay it in the morning. I've borrowed the money from Maudie.'

'Borrowed.'

'What else could I do?'

'But you still owe it.'

'I know, Sebastian. What is this — the third degree? Maudie says it'll do at the end of the month. She's all right till then. The only other person I could have gone to is your grandmother and I didn't want to ask her again. Not just yet, at any rate.'

'She's not exactly loaded herself.'

'I'm well aware of that.' My mother's voice was cool now. They're right when they say that money causes a lot of trouble. Lack of it, certainly.

'There is one other avenue we could explore,' she said slowly. 'Your father.'

'Torquil? He doesn't have ten p to his name.'

'Not according to Maudie. She heard he'd had a big win on the pools. Several hundred.'

'But you don't want to have to ask him for money.'

'No, I don't. You could though, couldn't you?'

'Now listen, Bella!'

'Now listen, Sebastian!'

Why do I always have to be the one who gets the

13

dirty work to do in the family? Sam says that's not true, she does her share. But she never gets sent on missions to Torquil.

'Anyway,' said my mother, 'you ought to visit your father more often.'

I felt like grinding my teeth, only every time I've tried it hasn't come off. I made do with going round to Hari's and sounding off. He lives a street away, in a large, comfortable, *tidy* flat.

'That shop will never pay your bills,' he said, 'even if the customers pay up. Couldn't your mother get a job somewhere?'

'What can you imagine her doing?'

He thought. Clearly, he couldn't see her tending the sick, like his mother. Or delivering the post. She'd meet a friend on the first corner, drop the sack and get into conversation and before long they'd drift off to have a cup of coffee and she'd forget all about the mail.

'I can't believe she is *so* scatty,' said Hari.

'She's a jolly good cook,' I said. And the more exotic the recipes the better. After a couple of lessons on Indian cooking from Hari's mother she could make onion bhajees and chicken biryani better than Mrs Patel herself.

'She could turn the basement into a restaurant,' suggested Hari.

'Oh no, I don't think that's a very good idea.' I had visions of me doing the waiting and Sam in the kitchen washing up. Our mother would make fantastic dishes and hang about between orders chatting to the customers who would all think she was marvellous and tell Sam and me so.

'I think you will have to talk to your father, you know,' said Hari. 'Especially if he has won money on the football pools.'

14

I decided to go on Saturday morning. Hari and I arranged to go for a cycle-run down the coast in the afternoon. I would be in need of a good blow of fresh sea air after bearding Torquil in his den.

And some den it is too! He lives in a small flat up a dark smelly stair. The lights always seem to be out and there's usually a stink of tom cat.

I fumbled my way up the three flights and banged on the door. The bell doesn't work. Nothing happened. My eyes were gradually getting used to the gloom. There are two other flats on the landing and the door of one was being opened, just a crack, on its chain. The old man who lives there is afraid of being coshed on the head. He peered out at me.

'Hi!' I said.

'What are you wanting?'

'My father.'

'He'll no be up yet, likely.'

I turned back to my father's door and banged again and rattled the letter box. I squinted inside but saw only more gloom.

'Hey, Torquil!' I yelled into the slit.

And then I heard sounds. Shuffling. Coughing. Yawning. I waited and after a couple of minutes the door finally opened.

'Good morning,' I said.

'Sebastian! It's you, son! Come away in!'

The living room was in a state of chaos. A different kind of chaos from what reigns in our mother's flat. In hers it's colourful and clean; here it was neither.

'Excuse the mess — I've been busy. Start spring cleaning today.'

He yawned. He looked pretty rough. Unshaven, hair on end, eyes like poached eggs. The sight of him annoyed me, yet I felt sorry for him at the same time. I always find it difficult to be with my father.

'I was out with a few friends last night, Seb old man, and we were a shade late getting to our beds, you know how it is. I'll get you some coffee.'

'No, don't bother.'

'Tell you what — we'll go out for breakfast. Hang on a tick till I get my duds on.'

He disappeared and I moved to the window. There wasn't much to see outside, only two women gabbing on the opposite pavement. But on looking over at the window directly across the street, I saw that a woman was watching me. When I looked at her, she drew back behind the edge of her curtain. Hearing a movement behind me, I turned. My father was back. He had shaved and put on a clean shirt and cravat and yellow corduroy trousers.

We went to a café a few minutes walk away. He was known there. He ordered coffee and two bacon rolls and paid in cash which obviously surprised the man behind the counter. So maybe he was in the money after all.

'It's nice of you to come and visit your old pa, Seb.'

Now I was embarrassed and didn't know how I was going to get round to mentioning what I'd come for. The man brought the coffee and bacon rolls and we ate and drank and Torquil called for more coffee and we talked about all sorts of things, like the subjects I was doing at school and his prospects for work.

'I'm in the running for a job at the moment. Think I'm in with a shout, too. Publisher's rep. Well, you know how I love books, Seb. The man and I got on really well. I'm just waiting to hear.'

Eventually, he asked after Bella.

'She's fine.' I braced myself. 'Except that she's short of money.'

'It's the devil of a nuisance, money. Bad business that about the fur coat. Think what we could have done with that lot! A thousand quid!'

'She can't afford to pay the telephone bill.'

'That's why I don't have a phone myself – the bills cripple you.' (He'd had his phone cut off six months before.)

'She needs money, Torquil.' I looked him straight in the eye and kept looking.

'I could let her have a tenner.'

'That wouldn't go very far.' I felt my face getting hot. 'We heard you'd had a win on the pools.'

'Did you now? News travels fast in this damned city.'

'*Did* you win anything?'

'Fifty quid. That's all, honest.' He pulled out his wallet. Inside were two notes, a ten and a one. He held out the ten to me.

'Keep it,' I said and got up.

We parted outside the café.

'Keep in touch, Seb.'

I nodded.

'Tell you what – we'll have an evening out together sometime soon. We could take in a theatre or a film, have a bite to eat afterwards. There's a good Chinese place round the corner. I'll call you, when I get the job.'

3

The Rag Trade

Sam

I know that the term usually refers to the *new* clothing business, not the old, but that's what we — Seb and I — call it nevertheless. It annoys our mother. 'Rag?' she'll say. (Of course I don't really think of the clothes as rags.) 'You kids don't know what you're talking about. You don't see materials of this quality used in today's clothes.'

'Thank goodness for that,' says Granny, who likes nylon and polyester and other man-made fibres. Easy to wash, drip-dry and Bob's your uncle, they're ready to put back on again! When I was small I used to wonder who this Uncle Bob was. Him and the Giddy Aunt. (Though I did have an idea who that might be since our father's sister fits the picture. But I'll tell you about her later.) 'My giddy aunt!' is another of Granny's sayings.

After Seb drew a blank with our father we had no choice but to ask Granny for the money to pay the phone bill.

'Is your telephone really necessary?' she demanded.

'Of course it is,' said our mother. 'Don't I rely on it for my business? It's my lifeline. How else would my contacts get in touch with me?'

'The question is,' said Seb, 'is your business really necessary?'

Our mother gave him a look that was meant to kill,

but Seb's not as easily wiped out as that. He gave her a long look back but said nothing more, not while Granny was in, at any rate.

Granny seated herself at the kitchen table to write the cheque for the telephone bill. She had to have everything just right. She was brought three different biros (different colours) until she found one to her liking. 'Who would write cheques in green or purple, would you tell me?' At her left hand my mother set a wee glass of port, her favourite tipple. She took a small sip before squaring up to the cheque book. For a moment we thought she was about to write. Then she looked up.

'This is the last time I'll be able to help you for a while, mind. I'm saving for my holidays.' She was going to Tenerife with her friend, Etta, who works along the street in the newsagent-cum-tobacconist-cum-sweet shop-cum-anything else they take it into their heads to stock, and is a widow like herself. We'd helped them pick their apartment. Kitchenette with breakfast bar, private balcony, pool and poolside bar, approximately two hundred metres from the sea. As soon as the booking was made Etta had gone off to make appointments for Solarium and Slendertone treatments which were to tan and trim her thighs for the beach and the poolside bar. I'd tried to egg Granny on to do the same but with no luck. She didn't care how white she looked and as for her thighs, she didn't intend to show them.

'How's Etta getting on with the Slendertone, Gran?' I asked, before I realised that she had been about to put pen to paper again.

'Sam!' Seb glowered at me.

My mother said, trying to sound sweet, 'Don't be distracting your gran now, Samantha.'

Granny settled against the back of the chair once

19

more. 'It's a waste of money, if you ask me. I can't see any difference in her. Those black cords she wears still look like stretch pants. Some folk can suit themselves how they throw their money about, of course. Unlike me. *I* have responsibilities.'

Our mother smoothed out the telephone bill so that she would not forget this one. Granny peered down at it, kidding on she's short-sighted, which she's not. She can see from one end of the street to the other and round the corner.

'How much did you say it was, Isabel?'

Isabel read out the figure loudly and slowly as if she were talking to a foreigner or a small child.

'That's three times the size of my phone bill. You must be calling Los Angeles.'

'Disneyland's a good source for rags,' said Seb.

Now I glared at him.

Granny gazed down at the cheque book for a moment, gave another little grumble and then the point of the biro hit the paper. I wanted to cheer. But didn't. I kept my mouth clamped shut until she had written the amount in figures and words and with a flourish, and after a suitable pause, signed her full name – Williamina McKettrick. Ina for short.

'That's awfully good of you, Gran,' I said.

'Yes, thanks very much, Mother. The business would fade away if we didn't have the phone.' Our mother didn't look at Seb. He'd been giving her a hard time recently until I'd told him to shut up. We'd had an argument.

'She can't go on with the business, Sam. Some business! It's probably costing *us* money.'

'It is not! Sometimes she makes money. And she loves it, Seb.'

'She'll end up in jail for unpaid debts.'

'We'll have to think of something.'

'Oh yeah? Such as?'

'I don't know. I haven't had time to think yet.'

Since then I'd been doing some thinking and talking it over with my friend Morag. With her being down-to-earth, I was hoping she might come up with some practical ideas. 'Leave it with me,' she'd said. 'I'll talk to Dad about it.' Her father's in Marketing. He knows about outlets and making a profit.

'I don't know what you'd all do without me,' said Granny.

'Neither do we,' I said.

'When you and Seb are working you can keep me in my old age.'

'You'll never be old, Gran,' I said and, in fact, I couldn't imagine it.

She put down the rest of her port and held out her glass for a refill. Our mother up-ended the bottle into it. We'd need to get another. There were some things we could do without but Granny's port was not one of them.

'Oh, by the way,' she said, 'there's a paper job going. Etta said to tell you.'

We'd had our names down for months and Etta had promised to give us 'preferential treatment' as soon as an opening cropped up. 'Well, why not?' she'd said. 'You two need the money.'

She was right about that. Not that that amount of money would solve all our problems but at least it would buy Seb and me our lunches and give us a bit of pocket money. Otherwise we had to rely on the odd hand-out from Granny or wait for our mother to have a bit of luck. That meant buying something dead cheap and selling at a big profit. It hadn't happened for a while.

'There's just one job, though,' said Granny.

'We'll share it,' I said quickly.

'You're on!' said Seb. 'We can do mornings or after-noons week about. That way we won't have to get up early every week.'

'It'll be good for the two of you,' said Granny, 'to have to get out of your beds at a decent hour.'

'It might even make men of us,' I said.

But Granny was softened by the port and didn't launch into her army song. Instead, she went all soppy and started recalling a boy she'd once walked out with, who had done a paper delivery. She'd wait for him behind the paper shop and chum him on his round.

'I hope he split the money with you,' I said.

'Oh, you and your women's lib! There are other things in life, my girl!'

'Never said there wasn't.'

My mother didn't join in. She considered herself liberated and so didn't need to discuss the subject. With Granny, anyway, it was a waste of time, she said; her mother had never done anything she hadn't wanted to do in life, had never been under anybody's thumb, male or female, had controlled all the family finances even when my grandfather was alive and working, but in spite of that she had a vision of a man as the strong leader heading the family and showing the way. That was why she hadn't taken to Torquil, my mother said.

We had to get up at six for the morning paper round but I quite liked it once I was out of bed. The streets were quiet and the air smelt fresh. Usually Morag chummed me on the afternoon delivery, which took longer since we blethered the whole way whereas in the mornings I'd dash up and down the tenement stairs taking two and three steps at a time. 'Like a young gazelle you are,' said a man who lived in a top flat, hanging over the bannister rail to watch me. I didn't much like the sound of that so in future threw his paper up the stair from the landing below. 'Catch!' I'd shout. One day I hit him full on the face, by accident, you understand, and after that he didn't bother coming out on the landing any more.

On the round, Morag and I discussed my mother's business.

'You know, Sam, I think Bella's prices are too cheap. I was in a shop in the Royal Mile the other day and they were selling those Victorian nightdresses at double what she charges.'

'Yes, but the Royal Mile's a different bag of beans. Tourists go there to unload dollars and yen. Our street's a bit more, well—'

'Downmarket,' said Morag, using a word that I never would, not about our street. 'Yes, I know. But I bet those dealers come and buy from Bella. And some tourists do come to our street. What we need to do, Sam, is to make a survey of the market.'

I shoved the last *Evening News* through the last letter box and we went back to the shop to hand in the sack.

'Won't be long now, Etta,' I said, meaning Tenerife. I took a quick look at her thighs and thought Granny might be right. The trouble with our granny is that she's too often right.

'Two weeks and three days. I'm counting them. Need to get this ball and chain off my back for a bit.' Etta looked over at the man who owns the shop but he wasn't paying any attention. He was busy putting out chocolate bars. He wouldn't give you one if you were passing out with starvation on the floor. Etta, now, she often slips me a wee bar when I hand in the sack. If he's not around, that is. And I eat it before I go home as my mother is anti-chocolate. She reads about it in her health magazines. Apart from rotting your teeth, it gives you brainstorms, or something.

Morag and I set out to do our survey of the rag trade on the Saturday following. She brought a notebook and biro with her. A black one. She was very businesslike, had the book set out with headings, such as nightdresses, underwear, shawls, etc., with a column for approximate age and one for prices.

We started at the top of the Royal Mile, just below the Castle, and worked our way down, planning after that to go through the Cowgate into the Grassmarket. In the antique and second-hand shops we jostled around with folk babbling away in a number of foreign languages. They were spending plenty of money and exclaiming with delight over tatty bits of lace and stained tray cloths that my granny wouldn't have used for dusters.

In one shop an Australian woman was looking for a Victorian nightdress. She couldn't find one she liked, so I sort of sidled up to her and said in a low voice, 'I can tell you where you can get an excellent selection of Victorian nightdresses.'

'Could you, dear?' said the woman back in a loud voice. 'That would be great. Can you give me the address?'

I did, and as soon as she had thanked me in an even louder voice and departed, we skedaddled too, for we were getting nasty looks from the woman behind the counter. Having sent a customer running downhill to our shop, or so we hoped (in fact, she did go and she did buy a nightdress, and a couple of other things besides) we decided it was time to refresh ourselves in a tea room. We had a Coke each and a piece of shortbread between us. The place was full of tourists with cameras slung round their necks and plastic macs over the backs of their chairs.

'I think you're right, Morag,' I said. 'We are going to have to put our prices up.'

The next shop we went to specialised in bedspreads and tablecloths.

'Look at this, Sam! A bedspread for sixty pounds!'

It was white, cotton, hand-embroidered in a thistle motif. We opened it up to see if it had any stains and it did, a big one right in the middle.

'That would easily wash out,' said the woman, who had on jangly earrings and looked a bit like a gipsy, but wasn't. 'Are you interested in buying a bedspread?'

'We're looking for my mother.'

'This is a beautiful piece of work. Mid-Victorian.' I'm sure she thought we didn't have two p to our names but was working on the principle that unlikely looking customers sometimes buy and so you can't afford to put them off. It's a principle we work on ourselves.

'I'll tell my mother,' I said.

Morag made a note in her book. Jangles craned her neck but Morag covered the page with her hand.

'That's a very nice blouse you've got on,' said Jangles, and reaching out her blood-red talons, she fingered my sleeve. I'd seen her eyeing it. It was in cream-coloured silk and had a high ruffled neck and ruffled cuffs. 'I might be able to offer you something for it.'

'Oh?' I looked at her round-eyed. (Or so I hoped.)

'Seven pounds.'

'Sorry. It's mid-Victorian.'

She changed her tune then, having thought at first, no

25

doubt, that I didn't know pure silk from pure polyester. 'Twelve,' she said.

'Twenty,' said I, not even having decided if I wanted to sell.

'Thirteen.'

'Nineteen.'

'Fifteen,' she said. 'And not a penny more.'

'Done,' said I. My mother had bought it for next to nothing along with a bundle of other things.

'What are you going to go home in?' asked Morag, ever practical.

'I'll find you something,' said Jangles and disappeared through her bead curtain into the back shop returning after a minute with a ghastly orange tee-shirt which looked as if it had been used as a duster. I hoped no one I knew would see me on the way home.

With the garment on my back (Jangles tried to charge me two pounds for it but I said, 'No way!') and the fifteen pounds in my jeans' pocket, I sallied out, followed by Morag who was still busily writing in her notebook.

The next shop had a quiet, hushed atmosphere and the woman didn't jangle at all. She stood very still, with her hands folded in front of her, and she wore round, gold-rimmed glasses.

'Can I help you, girls?'

'We're just looking.'

She looked at us looking, she didn't trust us as far as she could see us. She had one or two quite nice Paisley shawls hanging on the wall. I put up my hand to turn over one of the price tags.

'Seventy-five pounds,' she said right behind me.

Just then her phone rang and she had to go and answer it. It was round the corner in the back shop. She stood with one foot in the shop and one foot out so that she didn't lose sight of us.

'Fancy,' said Morag, 'seventy-five pounds and it's got a big darn in it.'

'That goes to show it's a genuine oldy-mouldy.'

'You wouldn't catch me wearing a darned shawl.'

'Honestly, Morag! You'll be like my granny in fifty years time.' Morag never takes offence. Or maybe she fancies ending up like my granny.

'Has Bella got any Paisley shawls?'

'One. She has it draped over a chair beside the divan that she sleeps on in the living room. Seventy-five pounds,' I said thoughtfully. My head was working like a cash register and the number seventy-five was ringing up on it loudly and clearly. 'Hers isn't darned either.'

The phone pinged. The woman had put down the receiver.

'Come on then, Morag,' I said, moving towards the door. 'I think I preferred that shawl we saw further up the street.'

We went down the hill and crossed Princes Street, swarming with Saturday shoppers, and descended into the part of the town which was ours. We told my mother that the stock had to be re-priced. Morag displayed the notebook and we didn't stop talking until she agreed.

'You can do the re-pricing next Saturday then, but go easy! I'm taking a run down into the Borders with Maudie. There's a sale in one of the big houses. I thought we'd make a day of it.'

We did go fairly easy with the re-pricing. Whenever I was tempted to skyrocket, Morag held me back. 'They've still got to *seem* like bargains.' And in the cupboard where things wait to be mended I came upon no less than six hand-worked bedspreads. My mother isn't really interested in bedspreads and tablecloths, it's clothes that

27

turn her on. Morag and I sat in the doorway in the sun and mended the spreads, doing stitching that Victorian girls might have been ashamed of but we weren't. We'd just finished when we saw the American coming. We knew he was a Yank because of the big cigar.

'Hi, girls! You're busy.'

It turned out that he was a dealer and, amongst other things, was looking for Victorian bed linen.

'I'll take the lot,' he said carelessly, as if he were talking about buying boxes of matches. I wasn't used to this big-time stuff. It took my breath away but I recovered it sufficiently to haggle with him over the price. In the end we agreed to two hundred pounds for the six bedspreads. Two hundred! I was feeling faint now. That should get us out of the red. And the bedspreads had been lying there for ages gathering dust.

He wasn't interested in the clothes, especially the ones in the forties and fifties style.

'Got any Paisley shawls, by any chance?'

'There's the one in your mother's room,' said Morag.

She waited in the shop with the Yank while I nipped across the road. I took the shawl off the chair and held it up to the light. The reds and blues glowed. It was a pretty nice shawl. Should I take it? Would Bella mind? But she hadn't touched it for years. It just lay there, and she threw her clothes on top of it when she went to bed. And I'd given the shirt off my back to help the family coffers. I took the shawl back to the shop and spread it out on the counter.

'Not bad,' he said and chewed on his cigar. 'How much?'

'A hundred.' Best to start high and come down if necessary.

'Done,' he said rather fast and took out his wallet.

He paid us in cash. After he'd gone we sat and admired the stack of twenty pound notes.

'Gosh, won't Bella be pleased!' said Morag.

She came home as we were getting ready to lock up. She had Maudie with her. Maudie is an aromatherapist, and her best friend.

'Hi, you two,' said Maudie. She smells of the aromas she works with, sort of sandalwoody and pepperminty and myrrhish. 'Had a good day?'

'Pretty good. Just had a Yank in who spent three hundred quid.'

'Fantastic!' said my mother. 'What did he buy?'

'Those six bedspreads from the cupboard — for two hundred.'

'Brilliant.'

'And you know that Paisley shawl of yours?'

'What Paisley shawl?'

'The one over the chair.'

She had gone awfully quiet and Maudie had stopped raking through the rack of long dresses.

'*You didn't sell that?*'

I was beginning to think I might be unwell shortly. 'Well, I mean . . . he did offer a hundred for it.'

'And did you sell it, Samantha?' She didn't really need to ask. 'Would it interest you to know that it is a *very* fine shawl and that it must be worth at least double that, if not more?' Her words peppered me like cold, sharp hail.

I couldn't speak and Morag was looking green, as if she might have to make a dash for the outside area.

'But that's the least of it,' went on my mother, 'for nothing would have persuaded me to part with it. Not even five hundred pounds. Or a thousand. For, you see, Samantha, your father gave it to me as an engagement present.'

4

Twelfth Night

Seb

My mother called me Sebastian after the character in Shakespeare's play. It's not a piece of information I usually give out, but when I met Viola, or rather when we got round to introducing ourselves, I did tell her. For, you see, her mother had done the same thing to her. I could hardly believe there was another mother like mine loose; though, in fact, Viola's mother is like mine only in this one respect. In all others, she is totally unlike. But totally.

She's an accountant and she wears neat suits with high-heeled shoes and her hair always looks as if it's just come straight out of the hairdresser's. Her husband, Viola's father, is a solicitor, with his own firm, well, naturally with his own firm, and he wears dark suits, striped shirts and black shoes. They live in a posh street of Georgian houses (ours is Georgian too, but Georgian as it was built for the workers) and they send their daughter, Viola, to a posh fee-paying girls' school.

Sam and I don't go to fee-paying schools but then you wouldn't expect us to. Even if my mother approved of them, which she doesn't, she obviously couldn't afford the fees. She doesn't approve of them because, she says, they segregate people and she believes that all people are equal. I believe that's the way it ought to be but when I look around me I don't see too much evidence of it. The other reason that my mother disapproves of private schools is that my father went to one. He was sent to boarding-school when he was seven. 'Look what it did to him!' she says. She herself went through the 'state system', as it's called; she didn't come from the kind of family where there was any choice. Torquil hated boarding-school, cried himself to sleep every night. He told me about it once when he'd had a drink or two. His family expected to send their children 'away' to school. 'Why have them in the first place?' asks my mother. My father's family are of the 'landed gentry'. Their land now consists of a few square yards of boggy ground surrounding a semi-ruined castle in Argyllshire. But that's another story and I'm not out to write about them at the moment, or fee-paying schools either, for that matter, but about Viola.

You might wonder how I came to know a family like Viola's. It was through the paper round. I delivered their papers, the *Scotsman* and the *Times* in the mornings, one week, and the *Edinburgh Evening News* in the afternoons, on the other. I preferred the afternoon round for it was then that I got to know Viola. In the mornings, if I left their street to the end, I might see her on her way along to the bus stop and she'd wave but she didn't have time to stop. In the afternoons, by timing it well, I 'bumped' into her coming off the bus on her way home from school.

To begin with, we didn't say much, just 'Hi!' or 'Wish the rain would give over' or 'Is that our paper? I'll take it for you if you like. Save you coming up the path.'— 'Thanks a lot. Been playing tennis?'

Sometimes she carried a tennis racket; at others, a musical instrument in a case. I couldn't quite decide what

32

instrument it was from the shape under the cover.

'Had music today?'

'A viola lesson.'

'So you play the viola?' (You see how scintillating my conversation was.)

'Uhuh.' She laughed. She has amazingly neat white teeth. I couldn't help wondering if she'd had them trussed up in a brace when she was younger, though I guess that wasn't a very romantic thing to be thinking. Bella had once tried to get Sam to wear a brace but it had ended up under her bed, in dark corners of the stair, anywhere but Sam's mouth. She'd hated it. 'My name's Viola, too.'

'That's a nice name.' I had known that her Christian name started with V for her initials are V.M.T. They're printed on the leather briefcase that she uses for carrying her books to school. I take mine in an old Adidas bag. I had been thinking her name might be Victoria or Valerie or Virginia but I hadn't considered Viola. Funny, really, that I hadn't thought about the Shakespeare play.

'My mother called me after Viola in *Twelfth Night*.'

'Really? My mother called me Sebastian because of *Twelfth Night*, too!' And for the first time in my life I was glad that she had.

We had a good laugh then, Viola and I. Imagine, Sebastian and Viola! Imagine! They were brother and sister in the play, of course, but we weren't in a play. I felt like quoting the first line to her, but didn't. I didn't know her well enough. I didn't really know her at all. So if I'd come out with 'If music be the food of love, play on' she might have run a mile, or at least the few yards up her garden path. I said it inside my head, though, and I imagined her opening up the case and

33

getting out the viola and sawing away on it right there in the street.

Instead, we talked. For ages. About school, mostly, and a bit about tennis. How we'd like to go to Wimbledon, and what a great player Becker was. We talked for so long that her mother came home from work while I was still there, leaning against the railings. It was then that I saw her suit and shoes and hair. She had her eye on me as she parked the car very efficiently in a small space outside the house. I straightened myself up and wondered if I shouldn't move along. I had a feeling she wouldn't think much of me. A paper boy! Not quite the thing for our Viola!

'Hello, Mother,' said Viola, going forward to kiss her cheek. 'Had a good day?'

'Busy, but good.' She looked questioningly at me.

'Mother, this is Sebastian. Isn't that funny — Sebastian and Viola?'

Viola laughed, her mother didn't. She smiled, but only with her mouth. How come, I wondered, that such a hard-faced woman could have such a sweet-faced daughter? Hard Face gave me a nod and went up the path, carrying a briefcase in either hand. At the door, she looked back.

'Will you be coming in soon, Viola?'

'In a minute.'

I was sure I had been branded 'unsuitable'. But maybe Viola paid no more attention to what her mother thought was suitable for her than I did to mine.

'I'd better go in and give my mother a hand,' she said. 'She has to work awfully hard. She's an accountant.'

The next afternoon we had an almost repeat performance, but with her father. He returned from work first that day. Parked his car. Got out with two briefcases.

Looked me over. Didn't like what he saw. Was introduced. I had a feeling he had heard about me.

'Your mother's going to be late, Viola. She would like you to start the dinner.'

'I'll be in in a minute.'

'Don't be long, then.' He gave me a nod and went off up the path with the two briefcases.

'Can't your father cook?' I asked.

'Cheese on toast. Boiled egg. Can your father?'

I was sorry now that I'd laid myself wide open to her asking questions about my father. 'He's not bad,' I said off-handedly. 'He's good with pasta and Chinese recipes. Anything out of the ordinary.'

'Daddy's got a fairly demanding job, of course. He doesn't have much time to do things like cooking. He's a solicitor. What does your father do?'

The dreaded question! I could hardly say he was a layabout. And that my mother, if Viola were to ask that, too, ran a second-hand clothes shop. Torquil, though, had done a number of things, if only for short periods, and I sometimes called them up. For example, he's done some acting, even went to Drama College for a year before being chucked out.

'He's an actor,' I said and hoped my face wasn't too red.

'How interesting! Would I have seen him in anything?'

'I doubt it. He hasn't been working too much recently.'

'Oh, he's resting, is he?'

'Yes — er, sort of.'

'Your mother then — does she have a job?'

'She has a sort of ... er, well, shop. She sells clothes and things.'

'A boutique?'

I nodded. I bent and picked up my empty paper sack.

That was as much cross-questioning about my family as I could take for one day.

'See you,' I said.

She waved goodbye to me from inside the gate. On the way back to the paper shop, I wondered how I could get round to asking her out. And for what? I didn't have much money to take her anywhere fancy. A walk, Hari had suggested. But how could you ask a girl like Viola who went to a fee-paying school and carried her books to school in a leather briefcase to go for a walk along the Water of Leith? I had not, of course, consulted Sam. Her advice, apart from the fact that I didn't want her to know anything about my private affairs, would not be worth having. She'd probably have suggested trampolining at Portobello.

> If music be the food of love, play on;
> Give me excess of it, that, surfeiting,
> The appetite may sicken, and so die.

(My mother likes to quote from *Twelfth Night*; that's how I'm able to quote from it too.)

I didn't think there was much chance of me getting a surfeit of love and so my appetite felt pretty sharp right then. You could even have said I was hungry. Starving.

Etta was ready to lock up.

'You're late.'

'I met a friend.'

'Do you meet her every afternoon, Seb? Got yourself a wee girlfriend, have you?'

To my annoyance, I felt my face heating up. My grandmother might be a sore trial — yes, one of her phrases — but her friends run her a close second. To change the subject, I asked about Tenerife.

'Five days, just! I'm getting fair excited.'

Granny wasn't letting herself get too excited. She doesn't believe in 'being carried away'. I felt quite carried away by Viola as I sat at the supper table half listening to Granny going on about her customers. At the end of a hard day she likes to let off steam so we usually get some of the spray on our faces.

'What's up with you the night, Seb?' she broke off to demand. 'You're not off your food, are you?'

'It's me that's off my food,' said Bella, turning her mournful gaze on to Sam. 'When I think that you actually *sold* my shawl——!'

'I've said I'm sorry, haven't I? About sixty times over!' Sam flounced off to the kitchen. We heard a clatter as she dropped — and broke — a plate. Talk about peaceful family meals! They're virtually unknown in our house.

After Sam and I had done the dishes — it was my turn to wash, hers to dry — I went round to Hari's. He was reading a book. He doesn't have to do dishes, his mother thinks it's 'women's work'.

'Did you see her?' he asked.

I gave him a report on my progress with Viola.

'Why don't you ask her to Duncan's party on Saturday night?' he suggested.

Duncan is a boy in our year at school. He has parties that never get out of control; his parents hang about the house to make sure they don't. It seemed like just the kind of thing to take Viola to.

'I'm taking Hilary,' said Hari.

'Oh, you are, are you?' He hadn't said anything to me about asking her. Hilary's also in our year and she's okay. She plays the violin and goes to France for her holidays. She and Viola might well get along together.

'Right!' I said. 'I'm going to ask her.'

The next afternoon I zipped through the round as fast

as I could, saving Viola's street till the end, as usual. I waited on the corner for her bus to come. When it did, she wasn't on it. I cursed a bit and went for a walk until the next one was due. What if she'd gone out with some other boy, one from a fee-paying school! There was no shortage for her to pick from. I'd all but convinced myself that she was sitting in a café with some stupid ass in a fancy blazer, when the bus arrived and there was Viola jumping off, swinging her tennis racket. What an idiot I was!

'Hi, Sebastian!' She almost seemed to expect to see me there. We walked along the road talking away as if we'd known one another for years. She'd been playing in a tennis tournament. And she'd won. Later, I wished that I'd said then and there, 'Let's celebrate!' and taken her for a Coke. But often you can't think what to say till afterwards.

We reached her gate. We stopped. She put down her briefcase and tennis racket.

Now! I told myself. I cleared my throat. I said, 'Viola—

And just then, a voice called, 'Hey, Seb!'

It was my dear sister Samantha. She was coming along the road towards us with her friend Morag, and the two of them were right-looking sights, as my dear grandmother would say. They were wearing shiny satin dresses that came down to their ankles, shoes that were higher-heeled than they could quite manage, and ridiculous hats like the Queen wears, with small veils pulled down over their eyes. Viola's eyes were nearly popping out of her head.

'Seb!' Sam shrieked again, as they drew nearer, and teetered forward to collapse half on top of me.

'This is my sister Samantha,' I was forced to say to

Viola. 'And her friend Morag.'

'You bring the paper on the in-between weeks, don't you?' said Viola.

'I didn't think you'd recognise me.'

'It's the hair.'

That sent Sam and Morag into a fit of giggles. Honestly! Talk about being given a red face! Mine must have been like the setting sun. It was a bad scene and I had to get away from it as fast as I could.

'See you,' I muttered vaguely in the direction of Viola, and made myself scarce. It was Friday afternoon. She might not be at home on Saturday afternoon and even if she was her parents might be too. I'd blown it now. Or rather, Sam had. I won't tell you what I said to her when she came home, but it was fairly strong and we ended up having a shouting match.

'Cut it out, both of you!' cried Bella. 'You're giving me a headache. When will you ever grow up?'

'Seb's in love,' sang Sam and tried to dance out of my reach but she didn't make it. I swiped at her with a rolled-up newspaper and caught her right across the ear.

'Beast,' she screamed. 'Pig! Chauvinist pig!'

I went round to Hari's. He has no sisters. Lucky Hari.

On Saturday morning, I had to do the shopping. Sam was 'working' in the shop, if you could call it that. And in the bread queue, whom did I see in front of me but Viola! I was so taken aback that for a moment I didn't know what to say. But the next moment I did, for I wasn't letting any chances go past me this time. The bread shop has a café attached to it.

'Fancy a cup of coffee?' I said, quite cool.

It was amazingly easy. She said yes and soon we were sitting side by side at a table, giving our order to the waitress.

'Two coffees.' Then turning to Viola, I asked, 'Would you like something to eat? A cake?'

'I'd love a piece of strawberry gateau. I'm mad about strawberries.'

'One piece of strawberry gateau,' I ordered. I love strawberries, too, but I didn't know how much they'd cost — quite a lot, probably, since they weren't in season yet and they'd have been imported from Spain or California.

When the cake came, Viola offered me a bite. 'Go on,' she said, 'try it.' She offered it to me on her fork. It tasted fabulous.

I was feeling pretty good now. She must like me, I told myself, she hadn't had to say yes to a cup of coffee. I would take her to Duncan's party and we would have a great time. And tomorrow, Sunday, we could go for a walk, the four of us, Hari and Hilary, Viola and I. Viola and I. I hoped I wasn't sitting there grinning like a jackass.

'Viola,' I began and then paused as the body of a woman loomed up alongside us blocking out the light. The woman, who was dressed in navy-blue and white spots, was broad in the beam and the top deck too, and she had tinted auburn hair.

'Sebastian!' cried my dear grandmother and dumped her shopping bag down on a spare seat at our table. 'I thought I recognised you, son. You don't mind if I join you, do you? All the other seats are taken and I'm fair in need of a wee cup to revive me before I go back to my work. Those shops are plain murder the day.' She looked at Viola and, naturally, I had to introduce them. 'Pleased to meet you, I'm sure, dear. He's a dark horse is our Sebastian.' And she gave Viola what is known as 'a broad wink.' You couldn't have got a much broader wink than that one.

I can understand someone running away from home and going to London. It's a long way from Edinburgh. As I sat there, sandwiched between Viola and my aged relative (but not aged enough), trying not to listen to what she was saying, I contemplated the advantages of life in the Far South. My grandmother was asking Viola what school she went to — 'I hear that's a very good school, hen' — and where she lived — 'That's a very classy street' — and even what her father did — 'A lawyer eh? My, my! You fairly know how to pick them, son!'

I was not at all surprised, therefore, when Viola gathered up her shopping and said she had to go. 'I'm making the lunch. We're going out for a run in the car in the afternoon.'

'So you cook too, do you, dear? That's *very* nice. You must be a great help to your mother. It's been a real pleasure to meet you, Viola.'

My grandmother and I turned to watch her walk out of the shop. There went my chances of asking her to the party. There went my chances of asking her out for anything.

'You can tell she's class, Seb. No side to her, though, I will say that. She's a lovely looking girl. And what a pretty name she's got, too — Viola. Most unusual.'

Luckily, my grandmother is not familiar with the work of William Shakespeare so at least I was spared her making some fatuous remark about *Twelfth Night* and Sebastian and Viola.

'I think I'll have a strawberry cake,' she said. 'They look very nice. Fancy one?'

I didn't. That was not the kind of food I was in need of.

5

When the Cat's Away

Sam

We were all exhausted by the time we got the holiday-makers off to the Canary Islands. Granny kept coming back up the stairs to give us yet another instruction while Etta sat outside in the taxi with its engine running. We had to remember to feed Granny's budgie, water her plants (some twice a week, some once), check her window snibs night and morning in case any burglars had been in in the meantime. . . .

'Your taxi's waiting,' said our mother, who was drinking black coffee and doing a five finger exercise on the kitchen table. It's supposed to help her to keep her cool.

'It'll be costing you a bomb,' I said.

'You'll miss your plane,' said Seb.

Granny disappeared and then re-appeared for the last time in the doorway in her beige-coloured polyester trouser suit with her flight bag over her shoulder.

'And mind you behave yourselves while I'm gone,' she said.

'Have a good time,' we yelled after her.

I ran to the window to wave them off. They twisted round in their seats to wave out of the back window until the taxi turned the corner of the street.

'They're away,' I said.

It felt almost like *we* were on holiday. I remarked on the fact.

'It does a bit, rather,' said our mother, smiling. She'd forgiven me by now about the shawl. She never holds grudges for long. She poured herself another cup of coffee. If Granny had been there she would have been telling her it was bad for the nerves. Never mind that strong tea has just as much caffeine in it! Granny doesn't believe that.

'When the cat's away,' I said softly.

'Now, Samantha,' said my mother, but she smiled, sort of to herself. She was having an idea. After a moment she told us what it was. 'Perhaps we should have a little party this evening, oh not a big affair, just something quiet. A few friends. It's ages since we had a party.'

Ages to my mother means something different from what it does to other people. Two or three weeks, a month at most.

'We haven't got any money,' said Seb, who was no doubt thinking about the few pounds he'd managed to stash away from his paper round towards a pair of trainers.

'We don't need money,' said our mother. 'Everyone will bring a bottle and I've got some bits and pieces in the fridge I can knock up into something. There's that pound of prawns Mr Murchie brought me a day or two ago.'

'Several days ago,' said Seb.

'They'll be all right, I'm sure they will.'

Famous last words, as our granny would say!

Mr Murchie is a dealer who does the antique shops in the street regularly and brings our mother delicacies of one kind or another, often fishy. Last time it had been a pair of Arbroath smokies. We'd never dream of asking him where he gets the stuff from, of course.

I came home quickly from school that afternoon, bringing Morag with me. It was Friday so there'd be no school next day. We set to and cleaned the flat and then went over to the shop to see what progress my mother was making.

By this time she had invited half the street, which was only what we had expected, and by the time she closed the shop she would have probably invited the other half as well. She and Maudie were drinking fennel tea together.

'Your mother gives such marvellous parties,' said Maudie.

'I don't really *give* them. They just happen. You'll be coming I take it, Morag? And bring your mum and dad too, if you want to.'

'I think they're already going out tonight,' said Morag hastily. Her parents would find some of my mother's friends just a bit too 'way out'. Women who don't wear chain-store clothes and men who wear earrings make them uncomfortable. Mind you, there'd be plenty of people there in 'regular' gear. The Quinns who live across the landing from us, to start with. He'd come in a suit and she'd have on a 'nice' dress and they'd have a whale of a time. She's a school dinner lady, he works in a brewery. And, yes, he'd bring some beer with him.

We shut up shop half an hour early. As my mother said, anyone who knows us knows where to find us. There was no sign of Seb – he'd be out on the paper round. Probably hanging round that Viola girl's house, if I knew him. Trust Seb to go for someone snooty like her!

We started on the food. I helped my mother with the

salads, Morag made cheese scones and angel cakes, which are what she likes to make.

'You're a grand wee baker, Morag,' said my mother, using one of *her* mother's lines.

Morag's cheeks turned pink. She's always pleased when my mother praises her.

'And now for the prawn and rice salad!' said my mother, going to the fridge.

'What an amazing amount of prawns,' said Morag.

'Yes, Mr Murchie is very good to me. He's coming tonight, by the way.' My mother pressed her nose into the bowl of little pink shellfish. 'I *think* they smell all right. What do you say, girls?'

Morag and I sniffed them in turn. They seemed to have a fresh enough smell and they looked okay. My mother ate one, decided she wasn't going to die and tossed them into a dish with some rice and chopped egg, herbs and dressing.

The food looked pretty good when we'd finished. My mother has the knack of making a little go a long way. We set the dishes out on the kitchen table, placing the prawn salad in the centre.

'The *pièce de résistance*,' said my mother.

Morag went home for her tea, Seb came in. He didn't seem in too good a mood and when I enquired whether Viola was coming to the party he tried to hit me over the head with a copy of the *Evening News*. It's always the same — when he's losing he resorts to violence. I told him so.

'That's enough!' said our mother, holding up her hands. 'We are not going to have a party with you two squabbling like infants. And if you want something to eat you'll have to see what you can find.'

Seb and I had beans on toast, she had a cup of black

coffee. Then I remembered Granny's budgie, so before I got dressed for the party — I was going to wear a 1920's style dress in oyster-coloured satin with black fringes — I went along to feed him.

'Hello, Charlie,' I said, lifting him out of his cage on my finger. 'Are you a good boy, then? Your mother's gone to the Canaries with your Auntie Etta — what about that, eh?' I laughed but Charlie didn't appreciate the joke. I filled up his feed bowl and gave him some water and put him back in his cage. We had offered to keep him in our flat but Granny didn't trust the Quinn's ginger cat who was accustomed to treating our home like his own. The Quinns have two other cats, a black one and a tabby, but they're home-birds.

'Home-birds eh, Charlie? Just like you. See you tomorrow.'

I had a quick look round but there was no sign of any attempted break-ins. The flat was tidy: the dishes had been washed and the tea towel hung on its hook and Granny's bed was made up, with its satin bedcover spread smoothly over the top.

'Enjoy yourself, Granny! We will, too.'

When I got home I found my mother and Seb rearranging the furniture in the sitting room. We would need all the floor space we could clear. By the end of the evening there'd be people in every room in the house, and the hall as well.

I went into the kitchen — and yelled blue murder! The Quinn's ginger cat was sitting in the middle of the table eating prawn salad.

'Get off!' I screamed. '*Off!*'

My mother and Seb came running in behind me. The cat looked up from the bowl, a prawn hanging from his whiskers, and stared at us with his goosegog eyes. Then he leapt off the table and went streaking towards the door.

'How did he get in?' demanded my mother. 'You must have left the front door open, Samantha!'

'I'm sure I didn't.' (But I had.) 'Anyway, there's not too much harm done.'

Ginger hadn't had time to do more than eat a smallish amount of the prawns and rice. My mother took a spoon and tossed the salad around, covering in the crater he had left in the middle.

'There,' she said. 'No one'll ever know.'

'But we do,' said Seb.

'A few cat germs won't hurt anyone.'

We must be immune anyway, I reckoned, for Ginger had eaten the top off our dinner on many previous occasions.

People started arriving at eight, and half the street did come, and Torquil.

'How did he hear about it?' demanded our mother.

But, as Seb pointed out, Torquil hears about anything it is to his advantage to hear. 'He's got ears like a hunting dog.'

'Don't speak like that about your father, Sebastian!' said our mother sharply, and swept across the room to confront Torquil – in so far as she could sweep across a room milling with people. She was wearing a long green satin dress. Mr Murchie, who was sitting on the floor in the corner drinking Mr Quinn's beer, said that she glowed like a pure flawless emerald. The things people come out with! But then he fancies our mother. Along with half the men in the street.

I pushed my way through the crowd after her.

'I do not recall inviting you,' she was saying to Torquil.

47

'You look beautiful tonight, Isabella.'

'You needn't think you're going to get round me with that soft soap!'

I heard Seb groan. He was right beside me. But, in fact, Torquil didn't seem to get around our mother that evening for she turned on her heel and went back to join the man she'd been talking to beforehand. This man had been brought by Maudie and was wearing a white silk shirt open half-way down his hairy chest and a heavy gold chain round his neck. I didn't like the look of him at all. He was full of himself, for one thing. But his name was Dave so I was pretty sure he wouldn't have much chance with my mother. She likes men to have interesting names – like Torquil! She was talking away to Dave, though, and laughing as if she found him fascinating. But that had probably something to do with Torquil being in the room.

Seb was not looking happy. Perhaps he was thinking about dearest Viola. Hari was at the party with Hilary which probably made Seb feel he'd missed out.

I went into the kitchen to see how the food was doing.

'Lovely prawn salad,' said Mrs Patel. She was wearing a fabulous orange sari with gold edgings. 'Did you make it, Samantha?'

'No, Mum did.'

'Ah, what a splendid cook she is! I admire her so.'

I realised I was hungry myself so I took some food, including a few of the prawns. I'm really fond of prawns and usually we can't afford them.

'Lovely party,' cried Mrs Quinn, waving to me as she went past in the hall.

Torquil came into the kitchen. He hadn't eaten all day, judging from the amount of food he heaped on his plate.

'How're things, kiddo?' he asked me.

'All right,' I said warily.

'You haven't been up to see me for a while.'

'I've been busy.'

'We must do something together, one of these Saturdays. What about a day out at the seaside?'

I wondered if he thought I was still digging on the sands with a bucket and spade. I said, icily, (my mother's good at that tone of voice) that I'd have to consult my diary.

'Not courting yet are you, Sammy old thing?'

Naturally my face went beetroot colour even though I ordered it not to. I said, 'Excuse me, I have to go and find Morag,' and left him to his supper.

After all the food had been eaten we put on music and everyone danced. Yes, everyone. My mother wouldn't take no for an answer from anyone, not Mr Patel, who tried to plead a sore foot, nor Mr Murchie, who had to leave Mr Quinn's beer and get up off the floor. The windows rattled and the floor vibrated, though that didn't matter since the people who lived below were up here with us. We really did have a good time and I even danced with Torquil, who, I have to admit, is a marvellous dancer. Like our mother. She gave in and danced one dance with him – the cha-cha-cha – and then the rest of us fell back against the walls and watched.

'They could have been professionals,' said Mrs Quinn. 'Taken part in "Come Dancing".'

'Bravo!' cried Mr Patel and led the clapping.

Some people left around midnight, others stayed until one or two. Everyone but Maudie had gone by half-past. Seb went to bed and Maudie, my mother and I had a cup of linden blossom tea and chewed over the party. It had been a success, we decided.

Eventually, Maudie couldn't stop yawning and got up to go. My mother decided to chum her down the stairs to get a breath of fresh air.

'We'll clear up in the morning, Samantha.'

I thought of the morning paper round, then put it out of my head.

Maudie and my mother went out, and not more than three minutes could have passed before the door burst open and they were back again. They looked as if they had seen a ghost.

'Sa-Samantha—' My mother was spluttering and her face had changed colour so that it was beginning to tone in with her dress.

'What's happened?' I cried.

'Ginger's dead. He's lying down in the bottom passage — and he's *dead*!'

'The prawn salad,' I said slowly. My stomach was starting to roll.

'Oh, my God!' said my mother, clutching her throat. 'Ginger must have been poisoned.'

'Poor old Ginger,' I said.

'But what about us? We might be poisoned, too. We probably are. I never should have used those prawns!'

Maudie demanded to know what we were talking about so we told her the story of Ginger and the Prawns and immediately she began to feel sick, too. My mother ran into the bathroom and threw up. Her face was ashen when she came back.

'What are we going to do?'

'Ring the doctor,' said Maudie.

My mother rang the doctor who said we would have to get ourselves up to the Infirmary straight away. Salmonella poisoning was a very serious matter. He thought it likely we would have to have our stomachs pumped out. And we would have to get everyone else who had eaten the prawn salad to hospital as well. I won't go into all the details of getting your stomach pumped out — for that was what *did* happen — but let me tell you it is *terrible*. It involves having a tube stuffed down your throat, for one thing. I only have to think about it and I start to gag.

Seb said that he got the worst end of the stick because he had the job of going round and knocking up all the other people who had been at the party and asking, 'Did you eat any prawn salad? If so, you'd better get yourself up to the Infirmary fast and have your stomach pumped out!' He hadn't eaten any himself, you see. But he only thought he got the worst end because he didn't have to go through the pump ordeal.

We assembled in the Casualty Department, we twelve prawn-eaters — my mother and I, Morag and Maudie, Mr Murchie and Dave, Mr and Mrs Quinn, Hari and Hilary, and Mr and Mrs Patel. There should have been a thirteenth — Torquil — but Seb couldn't rouse him. He had either fallen into a deep sleep or gone on to some other party.

'I hope he'll be all right,' said Seb. 'I feel quite worried about him. What if——?'

But at that moment I was worried only about myself.

They kept us in hospital for what remained of the night and released us mid-morning. We went home in three taxis. Nobody said much to anyone else. My mother kept her eyes shut. I thought of my paper round. Etta's boss would be fizzing but he'd just have to fizz. Thank goodness, at least, that Etta and Granny were somewhere in the middle of the Atlantic Ocean off the coast of North Africa!

When we got in, Seb made my mother and me a

pot of camomile tea. Camomile was soothing, said our mother. She said also that she was mortified. Absolutely mortified. To think she had served poisoned shrimps at her party! And had been the cause of all those good people having to undergo such humiliation.

'Anyone can make a mistake,' I said, remembering the shawl.

The doorbell rang.

'Answer that, Sebastian,' said our mother. 'And tell them we've gone to Siberia for a week-end break.'

But he returned with Mr Quinn who had news to tell. Mr Quinn had just been talking to the publican who kept the corner pub.

'On his way home late last night – just after two – he saw Ginger being knocked down by a taxi. He picked him up and put him in the passage but he didn't ring our bell because he thought we'd be asleep.'

'Ginger was *run over*?' said my mother, sounding as if she'd been hit on the head by a sandbag. 'You mean he died because he was hit by a *taxi*?'

We were still taking in the information with all its implications when our doorbell rang again. My mother repeated her instruction to Seb, about the week-end break in Siberia.

This time he came back with Torquil, who looked bright and breezy – well, for him.

'Morning, all! Lovely sunny day outside. Great party last night, Isabella.'

'Did you have any prawn salad?' she asked.

'Indeed I did. Excellent it was, too. I had two helpings.'

'And you haven't been sick?'

'Sick? Certainly not. I've never felt better in my life.'

6

The Gold Chain

Seb

Our mother didn't go out for a couple of days after the Prawn and Ginger affair and she wore dark glasses even though she was indoors. I think she imagines that people can't see her properly when she's wearing shades. I went over to the shop and tacked a notice to the door saying 'Closed owing to family illness'. I had adamantly refused to look after the shop myself. I didn't care that it was Saturday, the best day for business. I didn't care that some woman was coming all the way from Glasgow with a suitcase full of highly desirable Victoriana. She could have been coming from the moon, as far as I was concerned. Though maybe not, *not* if she was coming from the moon.... But I'd had enough of family business, of one kind and another, and was going to take myself off out of the street for the day. Or for whatever part of it that I could salvage.

As I pushed the last drawing-pin into the door, I heard feet on the basement steps behind me. Turning, I saw Dave, Mother's admirer. Or Gold Chain, as Sam had nicknamed him. He, too, was wearing shades and his shirt was still half-unbuttoned so that you couldn't miss the chain.

'Shop shut?' he said. (Brilliant observation! I wondered what my mother could possibly see in him.)

'Bella's not feeling too good.'

'In the flat, is she?'

'Yes, but I don't think she's up to seeing anyone.' It was a fairly strong hint to get lost but he was obviously not the sensitive type who takes hints. He said he'd wander up and see how she was. I hoped that when he heard he'd gone through all that agony at the hospital unnecessarily he might go off Bella. But even then I knew it was a hopeless hope.

I made my way up to the street where Viola lives. The blossom was out in the gardens, the sound of a lawnmower filled the air. It was a peaceful-looking scene and I couldn't imagine wild parties going on here and people being ferried to the Infirmary to get their stomachs pumped out. It was just as well I hadn't asked Viola to the party! What if she had eaten the prawn salad? Her father might have sued us for damages. He'd have had to accept satin nightdresses and feather boas for payment if he'd won. I grinned. I don't think he'd have been amused.

Viola's house looked dead. The gate was shut, there was no one in the garden, no face at any of the long windows. I examined the cars in the street, found her mother's, but not her father's. They must be away for the day. My spirits bumped down the last bit left for them to go.

Hari had gone out with Hilary. My mother would probably be tête-a-tête with Gold Chain. I walked up to the West End and hopped on a bus that took me out to the Pentland Hills which lie just outside the city. Once there, apart from thinking from time to time how nice it would be if Viola were with me, I felt better. The air smelt clean and fresh. I climbed to the top of Skidlaw and sat in the sun enjoying the view over Edinburgh and the Lothian plain.

Hunger, and the afternoon paper delivery, drove me down. I lingered at Viola's letter-box, easing the *Evening News* in as carefully as if it were a roll of tissue paper. I caught a brief glimpse of a strip of Oriental carpet and the lower half of a grandfather clock. The clock was ticking. Tick-tock, tick-tock. Slow and steady. Otherwise, the house was silent.

I went home.

'We're having simple omelets for supper tonight,' said Bella. 'That's about all our stomachs will be able to manage. David's going to be cook. He's marvellous at making omelets.'

So he had advanced to being David. Well, he wasn't half bad at omelets, I'll give him that. I wouldn't give him much more, mind you, apart from a sock on the jaw if I thought I could get away with it. But he's quite a bit taller and heavier than me. He did the cooking with a great deal of fuss, waving his arms about and demanding our attention throughout the whole procedure, from the moment of cracking the eggs onwards. I wondered if he might be an actor. When I asked my mother later she said he had been at one time, but the life had been too draining for someone of his temperament, and he was now an artistic adviser, whatever that means.

'The great thing is to have the oil at just the right temperature.' He waved the smoking pan in the air. 'Are you watching, Samantha?'

Sam, who was sitting curled up in a chair by the window reading, lifted her head and grunted, then dropped her eyes again.

The whipped eggs hissed as they hit the pan. Bella looked as if she'd never seen anything like it in her life.

She even pushed her shades up for a second.

'*Voila!*' cried Dave, turning out the first omelet. (I couldn't help thinking it was an anagram for Viola, then I thought what an idiot I was!)

'Bravo!' cried Bella. 'David, you are absolutely wonderful.'

They went on like that for most of the evening, being absolutely puke-making. Sam, who had been half-asleep for hours, went to bed. I said I'd better go and feed Granny's budgie.

'Sebastian,' began Bella, chewing the inside of her lip, 'David's had to leave his flat at short notice so I was thinking he might spend a few days at your grandmother's, until he finds something else.'

'At *Gran's*?' It was a wonder, with her long-range ears, that that good lady hadn't picked up the suggestion and come zooming in through the window, whirling her flight bag above her head. She'd have a few choice words to say to Gold Chain.

'Why not?' said my mother, who can ask the most amazing questions at times. 'The flat's empty, standing there doing nothing. David's landlord has had to take his flat back for his daughter who's got two young children and nowhere to go. She's left her husband who was battering her....' The story went on. I noticed a large, unfamiliar canvas holdall standing by the wall. Bella wound up, 'And so, really and truly, it only makes sense for David to stay at your grandmother's. There's no need for her to know, after all, is there?'

I shrugged.

'So you can take David along there now and show him where everything is. I think we could all do with an early night.'

There would be no talking her out of it, not that I

even had the chance to try, with Gold Chain standing there smiling that soft-soap smile of his. He needed it pushed down his throat.

'Shall we go, Seb?' he said, picking up the holdall.

'I'll see you in the morning, Sebastian,' said my mother. 'I'll probably be asleep by the time you get back.'

We didn't speak much on the way along the street, Gold Chain and I. He whistled softly to himself. I had an idea that he didn't like me any more than I liked him. We climbed the stairs to my grandmother's flat and I unlocked the door. He walked in, clicking on the lights as if he owned the place. He swung his holdall up on to the bed, on top of the pink satin bedcover.

'Better not do that.' I felt as if my lips had gone rigid. 'My grandmother won't like it if you mark her bedspread.'

'She sounds like a right old bitch,' he said casually and took a look inside the wardrobe.

'Don't you dare speak——!' I took a couple of steps towards him, my fists clenching.

'What's wrong, sonny? Don't you like me calling your granny a bitch?' He still had his soft smile on. 'And now are you going to run home and tell mummy? Only joking, Sebastian old pal. You take life far too seriously. Bella says you like to take the cares of the world on your shoulders.'

I felt betrayed. To think she had discussed me with *him*! He was unpacking his bag, putting his clothes into my grandmother's chest of drawers, moving her winter underwear around to make more room. If she could have seen him she would have had a heart attack. I thought I might be in line to have one myself.

'It's all right – I'll remove all my traces before I go.

57

And mum's the word eh? Grandmum, if you like.' He thought he was terribly amusing. 'No one need know I'm here.'

I felt like taking hold of the gold chain and tugging hard, until he pleaded for mercy and promised that he would go and never darken our door again, but, as I've said before, he was bigger than me.

I fed the budgie, then I left, slamming the door behind me.

Bella was in bed feigning sleep. I put on the light. 'Are you out of your mind?' I demanded. '*Are* you?'

She groaned and said, 'It's only for a few days. He's homeless.'

'What do you know about him? How do you know he won't clear out Gran's flat?'

'There's nothing worth taking.' My mother sat up. 'David's perfectly trustworthy, Sebastian. He's an old friend of Maudie's, she's known him for years. And you're just an old fusspot.'

In the morning, when I delivered Maudie's papers, I rang her bell. She came to the door, pulling on an orange and bright blue kimono. I think I'd wakened her – it was Sunday morning – but I didn't care.

'Seb!' She sounded groggy.

'Can I come in for a minute? I want to speak to you.'

She took me into the kitchen and put on the kettle. She gave me the choice of camomile tea or Nescafé. I took the latter, she had the camomile. The table was covered with dozens of small bottles – her aromas. I unscrewed one and sniffed. The label said marjoram.

'Good for insomnia,' said Maudie, yawning. 'Now, what can I do for you?'

'It's that man – Dave. Bella's let him stay in our grandmother's flat.'

'Really? She must be smitten. Of course she's very impulsive, is Isabella. As well as romantic.'

'She needs her head examined. Do you like him, Maudie?'

'He seems all right. I hardly know him.'

'You *hardly know him*?'

'No, I met him in a pub the other night, we had a few drinks and got talking and then I asked him to your party. I thought he and Bella might get on well together.'

Gold Chain was eating his breakfast at our kitchen table when I returned home.

'Got a paper for me, Sebastian old pal?' He held out his hand to take the papers I was carrying. 'I always like a good read of the Sundays.'

'I thought you were an old friend of Maudie's?'

'Not exactly old,' he murmured. He folded a page of the newspaper back.

'Didn't you say he had known Maudie for a long time, Mother?'

'I may have done,' she said, lapsing into vagueness, which she does when she doesn't want to answer. She began to read the colour supplement.

They started to read bits out of the papers to one another. I made myself a bacon roll and took it outside to eat it. I sat on the basement steps of the shop in the sun and thought about Gold Chain and wondered what I could do to get rid of him. I considered various possibilities, like putting rat poison in his coffee or arranging for him to fall under a bus or dropping a brick on his head from a great height, but rejected them all for practical reasons.

Hari came up the street then. He wanted to know if I felt like a game of football. I did. We went down to the park where some of our pals were already playing.

Every time I kicked the ball I imagined it was Gold Chain's head. Wham! And again! Wham!

'What's got into you today?' said Hari. 'There's no stopping you.'

I put in four goals.

I spent the rest of the day with Hari. His mother made a slap-up meal which took us an hour or two to eat. I ate so many chapatis that my stomach felt like a football. The Patels had recovered from their hospital outing and were philosophical about the whole business.

'These things happen,' said Mr Patel, smiling. (Not often, surely?)

'What a shame for your poor mother,' said Mrs Patel. 'How is she?'

'It's been a strain,' I said and decided I'd better go and see what the scene was back there.

Bella was alone: Sam had gone out with Morag and Gold Chain had taken himself off to his digs for the night.

'How long's he going to stay there?'

'Now, Sebastian, don't start!' She took off her shades and glowered at me.

The doorbell interrupted any further exchange.

'Go and see who that is,' she said. 'And whoever it is, I'm in bed asleep, having taken six sleeping pills.' She *was* in a twitchy mood.

The bell rang again.

'All right, all right!' I muttered, as I went to the door.

I opened it to see two policemen standing on the landing.

'We're looking for a Mr Michael Davis.'

'There's no one of that name here.'

'He's sometimes known as Dave. He wears a heavy gold chain round his neck. . . .'

'You'd better come in,' I said weakly. I led them into the sitting-room.

'Sebastian, I thought I told you—' began Bella and stopped, on seeing the dark uniforms.

'They're looking for Dave,' I said and could hardly keep the smirk off my face.

'There must be some mistake,' she said, turning pale and putting her shades back on. 'What's he done?'

There seemed to be no end to the things he had done, including house burglary, fraud, and confidence tricks. They had a photograph of him taken from the front and both sides. It was Gold Chain, without a doubt, and he even had the chain round his neck.

'So he's a con man!' I said.

'Oh, my goodness, I hope he's not raiding Mother's house!' cried Bella.

'Do you have a spare key to the flat, madam?'

Bella gave it to them. They asked if I would accompany them and we set off after one of them had called up the police station and asked for reinforcements. 'Just in case,' he said. I wondered what Gold Chain had in the holdall.

There was a light in Gran's sitting-room window. I pointed it out to the constables.

'So he's there. Now you stay well back, son. He might get violent.'

I ran up the stairs behind them determined not to stay so far back that I would miss anything. The leading constable stuck the key in the lock and turned it and then entered quickly, calling out, 'Davis, we know you're there!' There was no reply. Gold Chain might be lurking under the satin counterpane. The two policemen went charging in. The sitting-room was empty, as was the bedroom, and the bathroom, and the kitchen. But the kitchen window had been pushed half-way up.

'He's gone out the back! He must have seen us.'

I led the way now, out of the flat and down the stairs and through the passage that goes into the back green. It was not quite dark. The evenings are long in late May.

We saw him crouching by the back wall. The constables charged like bulls, closing in on him. He gave himself up without a struggle. I watched them take him, hand-cuffed, into the police car which had arrived in the street with its siren blaring and its blue light whirling. Granny's neighbours were out lining the street to see what was going on.

'Give my regards to your mother,' said Gold Chain as he passed me.

Like hell I would!

The holdall upstairs was found to be full of silver and jewellery, amongst which I identified my grandmother's diamond and ruby engagement ring. She always left it at home when she went on holiday in case it would be stolen.

The policemen came back to take a statement from my mother, who by then had recovered herself sufficiently to talk without trembling.

'I did think there was something a bit – well, suspicious about him, Constable, to tell the truth.' She didn't look at me.

When they had gone, she said, 'I wasn't *that* taken by him. After all, I hardly knew him.'

'Why do you think he wore that gold chain all the time, when it was one of the things that would give him away?'

My mother shrugged. 'Vanity, I suppose, Sebastian,' she said.

7

This Isn't Tenerife

Sam

We knew that *something* must have happened on their holiday the moment Granny and Etta came in the door. They didn't exactly jostle one another and bump elbows, the way Morag and I do when we're having a spat, but they almost did.

'Did you have a good time?' I got the question in first.

'Very nice, thank you,' said Granny.

'It was all right,' said Etta.

Mother and Seb and I eyed one another uneasily. Enough had gone wrong at home, enough to send our grandmother into a good-going song-and-dance act (wait till the neighbours told their tales, wait till she saw the darn in her bedspread!), without the holiday having been a wash-out as well.

'I've got a nice meal all ready for you,' said my mother. She had told them to come straight here from the airport and she would feed them. '*Coq au vin*, with fresh strawberries to follow.'

'Smells good, Isabel,' said Granny, sounding amazingly docile. She hadn't even asked yet what we'd been up to. She took a bottle of sherry from her flight bag and poured us all a shot. I rather liked the taste, drank mine quickly.

'That's all you're getting, young lady!'

So she hadn't become *that* docile. They say a leopard never changes its spots. That's one of her own sayings.

Etta refused a drink and sat with her legs crossed and her hands clasped over the top of her knees saying nothing in a very definite way.

'Did you have good weather?' I asked. I was dying to hear all about it.

'It was very changeable,' said Etta. 'One minute the sun would be out, the next the clouds had come up from nowhere. That's what it's always like in the Canaries, apparently.'

'I got quite a good tan,' said Granny, removing the jacket of her beige polyester trouser suit to show us the tops of her arms. I gazed at them. It was the first time I'd ever heard her brag about having a tan. Usually, she sniffs and says that folk who lie in the sun and grill themselves like kippers need their heads examined.

I turned my attention back to Etta who, it seemed to me, looked slightly paler than she had when she went away, though I couldn't tell about the thighs as they were hidden under her trousers. (Polyester also, but red.) Maybe she'd been ill. I almost asked, but thought better of it.

'Come on now and sit in at the table,' cried my mother in a jolly voice that doesn't come naturally to her. I could see she was quite thrown by this new version of *her* mother.

'Thank you, dear,' Granny was saying and sitting in at the table ever so demurely and unrolling her napkin and placing it over her lap. Her lips kept twitching as if they were about to break into a smile.

'It's nice to be back,' said Etta. 'There's nowhere to beat Edinburgh, say what you like.'

'Oh, I don't know,' said Granny. 'I like abroad.'

'I don't think I'd go again to Tenerife,' said Etta sharply.

'I would,' said Granny.

I had to keep turning my head from one to the other like you see them doing at Wimbledon.

Seb asked what Tenerife was like and Granny launched into a long, detailed description of the flowers and the beaches and the mountains and the sunsets. The *sunsets*, for goodness sake!

'Oh, they were rare, those sunsets! You'd have thought the Atlantic Ocean was on fire.'

Etta sniffed. Seb, Mother and I exchanged looks again. Could our grandmother have had some kind of brainstorm?

'What about the apartment?' I asked. 'And the poolside bar?'

'First class,' said Granny.

'Not too bad,' said Etta.

'Well, I'm glad it all went off so well,' said my mother brightly and brought out the strawberries. I could see her thinking that maybe everything was going to be all right after all. Maybe Granny wouldn't even notice the darns in the satin bedspread. We'd found two holes in it, clearly made by cigarette burns. Maudie, who is very good at invisible mending, had done the darning but, even so, the stitches were quite visible. Especially to someone with sharp eyes.

'There was a very nice type of person staying at the apartments,' said Granny. 'Of course, it was a pretty classy place.'

She went to the bathroom while the coffee was being made and as soon as the door had closed behind her Etta gathered herself together and said in a throaty whisper, 'I think I'd better tell you, Isabel—'

'Tell me what?'

'Yes, what is it, Etta?' I cried. 'Tell us!'

'Well, the very first day we were there, we were sitting at the poolside bar, getting acclimatised, as they say, and drinking Tequila Sunrise—'

'What's Tequila Sunrise?' I asked.

'Never mind,' said Seb.

'Go on, Etta,' said our mother.

'And this man comes up—'

'A man?'

'Yes. A butcher.'

'A *butcher*?' I said.

The door opened abruptly at our backs and we almost fell inwards on top of the empty strawberry dish. I bumped my head against Seb's.

'I think it's time we were getting on our way, Etta,' said Granny. 'No, I won't wait for coffee, Isabel. It'd just keep me awake.'

'You didn't think that in Tenerife,' said Etta.

'This isn't Tenerife. Are you coming?'

'I thought I'd give Isabel a hand with the dishes.'

'She's not needing a hand. She's got Sam and Seb.'

The two ladies left together, with our grandmother saying she'd see us in the morning. She'd pop in as usual on her way to work.

'She must be in love,' I said.

'Don't be ridiculous, Samantha!' snapped my mother, who probably didn't like the idea of anybody being in love after what had happened with Gold Chain. 'At *her* age!'

I reminded her that Mr Smellie along the street had got married last year at the age of seventy-five. And his bride had been seventy-two. We'd all gone to the wedding and had a great time.

'There's no question of your grandmother getting *married.*'

'If he's a butcher we might get cheap mince,' said Seb.

Our mother, who would have nothing to do with red meat, gave him a look that was meant to wither. He just grinned. He seemed to be enjoying the situation. I pointed out that the butcher might live in Tenerife and if so they would have a job to go on seeing one another. Our mother said she hoped he lived on the Arctic ice-cap.

I resolved to ask Granny point-blank in the morning but didn't get the chance for the first half-hour. She had a lot to say to us. She might be in love (*could she really?*) but that hadn't blinded her to the darns in her bedspread or the chip in her favourite cup or the dirty mark on her bedroom wall that we must have missed. We'd spent the best part of a day spring-cleaning. Also, Granny's neighbour from across the landing had been in, and the one from the flat below, and Mrs McWhirter from over the street, and they'd had fine tales to tell!

'I might have known I couldn't go away and leave the three of you on your own! Imagine – a common criminal living in *my* house, sleeping in *my* bed, drinking out of *my* cup....' She stood throughout her tirade, shaking her head at her daughter waving the teapot in front of her, and at her grandson holding out a chair. 'I'm fair mortified,' she declared, in conclusion, 'to think that the police ran down a criminal in *my* house!'

'But what about the butcher, Gran?' I asked, now that she'd paused for breath.

'*What* butcher?'

'The Tenerife butcher?'

That had taken the wind out of her sails. (Another of

67

her own expressions.) She said, 'Has that Etta been opening up her gob?'

'Does he live in Tenerife, Gran?'

'No, he does not. He lives here in Edinburgh.'

'In Edinburgh?' we chorused.

'Are you planning to – well, go on seeing him?' asked our mother.

'And why shouldn't I?'

'Never said you shouldn't. Why don't you bring him to supper some evening?'

'Well, I might. I'll have to see.'

'Bring him this evening, Gran,' I said.

'Mr Murchie brought me in some nice fillets of sole yesterday,' said Bella.

Granny was still considering. 'Do you think I could count on you all to behave yourselves?'

Of course! we cried.

'No dressing up in any of yon rubbish from the shop, mind!'

Of course not! we cried.

'Well, all right then,' she said, not too enthusiastically.

I put on a blue skirt and a white blouse. My mother dressed in black. Granny brought the butcher along around seven.

'This is Hughie,' she said, sounding kind of stiff.

'Pleased to meet you, Isabel,' said Hughie, pouncing on our mother's hand and keeping hold of it. He eyed her dress. 'Nobody's died, I hope?' He laughed and looked at Granny who smiled back at him. Yuck!

'Not as far as I know,' said our mother in her chilly voice and removed her hand.

Hughie came up only as far as Granny's shoulder and he was about half as wide. A mere slip of a man, as our mother said later. I found it difficult to imagine him wielding a chopper but when I looked at his hands I could. They were surprisingly square and fleshy.

We didn't mind what height or width he was but we did mind about his conversation over the supper table. It was all to do with the butchery business, the price of rump steak and tripe and liver and kidneys and tongue. My mother's face was beginning to look greenish.

'I'm virtually vegetarian,' she said. 'I only eat a little white meat very occasionally.'

'You one of the Fruit and Nut brigade?' He gave us another of his laughs which made us feel he thought he was one of the all-time great comedians. Granny smiled again as if she thought he was the bees' knees. 'There's nothing like a good juicy rare steak to set you up. The blood should ooze out when you cut it, what do you say, Ina.'

'Oh, I like my meat right enough.'

'Yes, I know you do,' he said and patted her on the forearm which gave her a red face. Then he pushed aside the rest of his *sole veronique* and asked if we'd mind if he smoked, and without waiting for an answer pulled out a packet and lit up. He blew smoke across the table. My mother coughed as if she were racked with some dreaded lung disease but he didn't appear to notice. He carried on talking about meat prices.

'That reminds me.' He got up from the table. 'I brought you a present, Isabel.' He produced a carrier bag that he'd left by the door. 'A nice piece of pork with crackling and some best lamb's liver.' I thought Isabel would gag trying to say thank you. 'The liver'd do you good, bring some colour into those peely-wally cheeks.' He tweaked them with his square fleshy fingers. The marks remained on her skin for several minutes afterwards.

After Granny had taken Hughie away, we pushed the

windows up as high as they'd go to air the place out. Mother counted ten stubs in the ashtray.

'What a ghastly man!'

'We might have to have him for a step-grandfather,' said Seb cheerfully.

'Over my dead body!' said our mother and went round to Maudie's to tell her troubles and have her temples massaged with peppermint essence.

I went round to see Etta who was at home watching the telly. I told her what we'd thought of Hughie.

'What can she see in him?' I asked and remembered Bella saying once that no one could ever see what someone else saw in a person they were in love with. (After all, there was Seb all moony about that stuck-up girl Viola!) Or as Granny would say, one man's meat.... Ha, ha! At least that made me smile. 'She can't be in love, can she?'

'Search me! They were as thick as thieves in Tenerife anyway. Went everywhere together, arm-in-arm. You should have seen them! At their age!'

'Did you get left on your own, then?'

'They asked me to come with them but who wants to play gooseberry, would you tell me?'

Our living room still smelt of cigarette smoke in the morning. Granny didn't appear.

I went to the supermarket after school. She was stacking up wire baskets.

'Will you be coming round this evening, Gran?'

'No, not this evening, hen. I've arranged to go to Hughie's. I'm going to cook him a nice wee supper.'

'Tripe?'

'No, steak and kidney pie. That reminds me.' She went to the deep freeze and took out a packet of pastry.

The next night she made him lamb stew with carrots

70

and onions and the next, pork chops with apple sauce.

'This is beginning to look serious,' said our mother, frowning over the top of the extra-strong cup of coffee which she held between her hands. 'Especially since she hates cooking.'

On Saturday night Morag and I met Granny and Hughie coming along the main road arm-in-arm. They had been to the pictures.

'We're just on our way to the chipper,' said Hughie. 'Would you girls fancy a fish supper or something?'

We'd been feeling hungry and bemoaning the fact that we'd no money. I wasn't for accepting his offer but Morag jumped in and said that'd be lovely. I was going to say I didn't feel hungry but when I got inside the chip shop and smelt the chips I didn't feel strong enough to go through with it. I saw Viola in the queue and was surprised at that. I thought she'd be too toffee-nosed to go to the chip shop. Granny recognised her, too.

'Oh, hello there, hen. You're Sebastian's wee girl, aren't you? What's your name again? Violet?'

'Viola.' She was blushing. And no wonder! With Granny calling her Sebastian's wee girl! Viola gave us an uneasy smile and took her brown paper parcel. 'Cheerio!' she said. Wait till I told Seb! He'd kick himself at having missed her.

We ate our fish suppers going along the road. I couldn't get over Granny doing that — she usually says it's bad manners to eat in the street.

'Will you be coming to Sunday lunch tomorrow, Gran?' I asked.

'Aye, maybe I will. I haven't seen the three of you for a bit.'

'Are you forgetting, Ina?' said Hughie. 'You were

going to cook us a roast with all the trimmings? I've got a nice big piece of sirloin in.'

She looked at him and then at me.

'I think Mother's expecting you.'

'But you promised me first, didn't you, Ina? Didn't you?' he repeated and took hold of her arm. As if he owned her! I felt like taking hold of her other arm and dragging her away.

'I suppose I must've, Hughie.' Granny didn't sound too over the moon.

'Well, then!' he declared triumphantly. He seemed to think that that settled it. Granny was amazingly quiet. Surely she wasn't going to let a bully like that squash her!

Morag and I said we'd see them later and left them. I let off steam.

'He's not *that* bad,' said Morag. 'He did buy us fish suppers, after all.'

'Anyone could buy you off! We *all* think he's ghastly.' I ran up my stair wondering how I could be so friendly with someone as dumb as Morag.

We didn't see Granny for a couple of days and then one evening I thought I'd go along and try ringing her bell. Surely she couldn't be out with Hughie every night of the week!

I found her in. She'd been watching the television, she said, going back to her favourite chair and letting herself sink down into it. She kicked off her shoes and put her feet up on a stool. She'd been run off them at the supermarket, she said. It had been murder from lunchtime onwards.

There was a wee glass of port on the table at her side. She took a sip and sighed with pleasure.

'Have you eaten?' I asked.

'I bought a carry-out from the Chinese. I fair enjoyed it.'

'Granny—' I decided to plunge in. 'Are you going to marry Hughie? Because if you are—'

'Hold your horses, madam! He *has* asked me to marry him—'

'He *has*?'

'And I've thought about it.'

'And?'

'Well, you see, Sam, it's different when you come home from what it was on holiday.'

'Not so romantic, you mean?'

She nodded. 'And I've got my own wee place here, after all, and I like having it to myself and being able to do what I want, whereas Hughie doesn't like being on his own. He's been a widower for two years now. What he's looking for is a housekeeper, someone to cook his dinner and wash his socks.' She took another sip of port. 'He's not a bad soul – but I'm not for hire!'

8

Just my Luck

Seb

It was just my luck. Everything that happened that Saturday. The seeds were sown a couple of days before. I was sitting by the window reading a book on astronomy, minding my own business, and not wanting to have anything to do with anyone else's, when Bella and Sam came in.

'Sebastian, dear,' Bella opened up and I knew that something was coming that I wouldn't want to hear.

'Well?'

'Samantha and I have to go to Perth on Saturday.'

'I'm not minding the shop on my own.'

'We *must* go to Perth.'

'The answer's *no!*'

'We've got a lead on some fantastic stuff and Maudie can't take me in her car so I'll have to go on the bus and I'll need Samantha to help carry—'

'Shut the damned shop!'

'I do wish you wouldn't swear, Sebastian, at least not in front of me. We can't shut the shop – some Americans are coming. We need the money.'

'We always need money.'

'Naturally, if we want to live. And your grandmother's short after her holiday so we can't expect any help from her.'

She was back to being her old self again, was our grandmother, as if Hughie the butcher had never been.

'I'm sorry,' I said firmly. 'But I'm playing tennis with Hari.'

'Bully for you!' said Sam. 'Off out enjoying yourself while we slave our fingers to the bone.'

'Some slaving, going on the bus to Perth!'

'You can get Hari to help you.'

'Look, I am not minding the shop! I'm not going to stand there selling *women's* clothes.'

'Sexist!' cried Sam, which caused me to throw my book at her. She ducked and it hit the wall, doing damage to its spine. I picked it up and straightened it out and cursed.

'Nobody cares about these things nowadays, Sebastian,' said Bella, ignoring that interlude. 'Anyway, we don't just sell women's clothes. We sell tablecloths and bedcovers. . . .'

They wore me down in the end, got me against the wall. I had to surrender. Our electricity would be cut off, our gas, our telephone, there'd be no food to put in our mouths, Sam and I would be taken into care — if the shop was allowed to close on a Saturday in June.

'The town is full of tourists,' said Bella.

'Probably won't take ten p,' I muttered and went off to tell Hari, who was much less put out than I was.

'That's all right. We can play tennis later. It's light till late.'

On Saturday morning Bella and Sam set off for the bus station in high spirits. They love days out. Before they went they gave me reams of instructions and told me to watch out for shoplifters. Though who would want to lift any of that stuff was beyond me. Hari turned up at ten which was our scheduled opening time.

'We won't open till eleven,' I said. 'Nobody ever opens up when they're meant to round here. And at lunchtime we'll go for that game of tennis.'

There were three girls waiting on the basement steps of the shop when we went down to open it. But they didn't seem to mind. It was sunny and they were sitting with their faces turned up towards the sky trying to get a tan. They didn't seem surprised to find Hari and me in charge, they just surged in and began raking through the racks. They didn't look at all like shoplifters, though Bella had said you couldn't always pick them out. These girls were about seventeen or eighteen and they laughed a lot — and no wonder! They held various garments against themselves and asked one another, 'What about that?' then they'd double up and Hari and I would make faces at one another. They tried on half the stock in the tiny 'fitting room' (a cupboard, in other words), all three in there together. It must have been stifling.

Then they said, 'Thanks a lot' and drifted out, without buying a thing.

'If you ask me,' said Hari, 'Bella's shop provides good free entertainment.'

He could say that again!

'Do you think we should tidy up after them?'

I supposed so. The racks were in a heck of a mess, with coathangers half in and half out and some of the clothes lying on the floor. I closed the door firmly and took a look up the steps to make sure that no one was coming then, with Hari, did a quick clean up. We'd just stuffed the last dress back on the rail when the door opened at our backs.

'What are you two doing here?'

Two girls from our class in school had come in, Olive and Carol. They didn't laugh. They were just interested.

We talked to them for quite a while and I began to wonder if I shouldn't ask Olive to go out with me. It was a pity Hari was still going with Hilary for we could have asked them together and gone out in a foursome. Olive was talking about a film she'd like to see.

'Sounds good,' I said.

She smiled at me in what seemed an encouraging sort of way and I felt my face getting hot. Stupid ass! I told myself. I didn't know what else I could say then, not with Carol standing there too.

Olive bought a gloppy-looking pink blouse and they left saying they'd be seeing us.

'They're okay,' said Hari.

'Not bad,' I said, still annoyed with myself.

'Seen Viola recently?'

I shrugged. I'd seen her in the distance with another girl and nipped round the corner and waited until they'd passed.

The Americans did turn up, to my surprise, and they spent two hundred pounds, which would more than cover the current bills.

'Just as well we did open up,' said Hari.

We could trip off for our game of tennis now, though, I reckoned, so I selected from a number of pieces of paper bearing messages like 'Back shortly' and 'Gone for lunch' one that said, 'Back in ten minutes'. That seemed to me to be more likely to persuade potential customers to hang on.

We went to the public tennis courts and had to wait for a court. We lay on the grass and almost fell asleep. We had a good game – even though Hari did beat me! He's a bit of a whiz on the court.

We bought chips for our lunch and walked back to the street eating them.

'I think there's somebody waiting,' said Hari.

There was a girl on the steps peering into the shop window. Her back looked vaguely familiar. She turned round. It was Viola.

I almost choked on a hot chip. I spluttered and Hari thumped me on the back. My first instinct was to walk straight past as if the shop had nothing to do with me but I didn't get the chance, for Hari was already slowing up and smiling at Viola and saying he was sorry if we'd kept her waiting. He can put on the patter for women, can Hari. He's much better at it than I am.

'That's all right,' she said, looking puzzled. Looking at me.

I didn't know what to say. If I could have done a disappearing trick I'd have done it then. I just stood there like a dummy holding my bag of chips. I'd be stinking of the chips, and of vinegar and sauce. 'Lots of sauce,' I'd told the man and he'd sloshed it on. And there stood Viola in front of my mother's boutique. Some boutique! My face might have been hot when Olive was in, but now it was roasting.

'Hello, Sebastian,' said Viola.

'You know one another?' said Hari.

'Hari,' I said, 'this is Viola.'

'Viola!' whooped Hari, unnecessarily joyfully, I thought.

'Hello,' said Viola.

'Perhaps we'd better open the door, Seb,' said Hari.

'Have *you* got the key?' asked Viola, watching me produce it.

'It's my mother's shop,' I said and marched down the steps past her, without looking sideways.

I didn't look at her when we were inside the shop, either. I busied myself through the back sorting – or pretending to sort – bundles of old tablecloths. Hari was engaging Viola in conversation. They were discussing Wimbledon. Maybe he would get off with her. They could play tennis together all day long.

I heard the shop door opening again, and peering through a crack in the curtain, saw a man and a woman coming in. They were in their twenties. He had sideburns and pinched-looking eyes, she had blond hair that was growing out and her face was covered with make-up that looked as if it had been laid on with a trowel. They were both wearing jeans. She carried a beaten-up flight bag over her shoulder. I can still see them clearly in my mind's eye, could give a good description to the police if I had to. They began going through the racks. Hari and Viola went on talking, getting more and more animated and laughing like drains.

It took me a full minute to realise what was going on. The man and woman were lifting dresses from the racks and stuffing them into the flight bag. They had wasted no time. They were working quickly but coolly, without a trace of expression on their faces.

'Stop!' I cried, and went lunging through the curtain.

Immediately, but without seeming to panic, they turned and ran, slamming the door in our faces, and pelted up the steps. I followed, and Hari came after me.

They were wearing runners, the thieves, and they were practised in running. But I knew we could catch the woman, at least. She was beginning to fall behind the man. And Hari and I had been out training every evening for the past few weeks.

'Stop thief!' I shouted, and some people on the pavement stopped and looked round, getting in the way of the escapers and causing them to swerve. We nipped out into the road, dodged round a couple of parked cars.

We were narrowing the gap.

We caught the woman just before she turned the corner. The man had already disappeared round it. She chucked the flight bag at us. It caught Hari in the stomach, winding him for a second. I grabbed her.

She struggled like mad, kicking me in the shins and clawing my face. Her nails tore at my cheek, making me gasp, and I knew she'd drawn blood. Hari came up behind her and trapped her hands. She spat at him.

'Black skunk!'

'Take that back!' I bellowed, my temper now really up. 'If you don't we'll get the police.'

We'd collected a small crowd.

'What's going on?' asked a big bruiser of a man who'd come out of the pub. He looked as if he'd just put a few pints under his belt.

'Get them off me!' she screamed and the man stepped forward. 'They attacked me,' she shouted. Another man was moving in our direction, too.

For a few seconds I thought we were going to have a really nasty scene on our hands. I had visions of Hari and me getting beaten up and the woman escaping.

'She's a thief,' said Hari. 'Look in that bag.'

A woman picked up the flight bag and pulled out a jumble of clothes. Women's clothes.

'They're mine,' said the thief, who had gone passive in our hands but was waiting, I sensed, for the right moment to tear herself free.

'She steal them from you lads?' asked the bruiser and grinned. But he didn't grin in a friendly fashion. And he came closer.

'They're from my mother's shop.' I could now feel the man's breath on my face.

'Leave him alone,' said a woman's voice sharply from

the edge of the crowd. It was Mrs Quinn. 'He's telling the truth. His mother has the second-hand clothes shop in the basement along the street.'

The man hesitated, then shrugged and turning, pushed his way back out of the crowd.

Hari and I still held the woman. But we couldn't hold on to her for ever. I said, 'You haven't taken it back yet.'

She arched her neck back and laughed. 'You mean about the black——? Oh, I do beg your pardon, I'm sure.'

'Let her go,' said Hari and took his hands away. Then I let go. She sprinted through the crowd, almost knocking Mrs Quinn and another woman off their feet. I shouted after her.

'Don't ever show your nose round here again, you stupid bitch!'

We walked slowly back along the street after Mrs Quinn had had a look at my face and asked if I was all right. I told her I was fine, though I didn't feel it. Both Hari and I felt quite shaken by the incident.

'People like her aren't worth bothering about,' he said.

I suddenly remembered the shop. Half a dozen shop-lifters could have been clearing it out while we were away. We ran the last few yards.

But I needn't have worried for there was Viola (whom I'd also forgotten) standing behind the counter serving!

'It looked very good on you,' she was saying as she put something into a bag. 'I'm sure you'll enjoy wearing it.'

'Thanks, dear,' said the customer and went off up the steps.

'Sebastian!' cried Viola and bit her lip. She was frown-ing at my face. 'What's happened to you? Are you all right?'

'I'm fine,' I said and this time I meant it. My cheek

had miraculously stopped stinging and the woman thief was beginning to fade into the distance, where she no doubt was by this time.

Viola came out from behind the counter to take a closer look at my injury, but I said that it was nothing and paid no attention to Hari, who was wanting me to go through to the back shop and get my face cleaned up.

'It was good of you to mind the shop for us while we were gone, Viola,' I said.

'Not at all. I enjoyed it. I love old clothes.'

'You do?'

'Oh, yes. I find them far more interesting than new ones.'

Another two customers came in and Viola said she would look after them while I let Hari tidy me up. He'd been doing a First Aid course and was desperate to have someone to practise on. He and I went into the back and he dabbed at my face with a piece of rag (no shortage around here!) soaked in cold water and I winced and tried to get out of his reach.

'I'm going to ask her out, Hari! Tonight!'

'She's nice.'

'I told you she was.'

As we went back into the shop the door opened again and who should come in but Olive! She was wearing the gloppy pink blouse. There was no sign of Carol.

'Seb,' said Olive, coming straight up to me, 'I meant to ask you earlier but I forgot. I wondered if you'd like to come to Jane MacKay's party with me tonight? Hari's going with Hilary, aren't you, Hari?'

'Yes, I think so,' said Hari, sounding uncomfortable. 'Yes, I am.'

Olive was looking at me and waiting for an answer.

I felt as if my tongue was stuck to the roof of my mouth. My wound had started to smart again.

Behind us, Viola moved. She came out from the back of the counter.

'I'll need to be going now,' she said.

'Thanks very much, Viola,' said Hari.

'Oh, yes — er, thanks,' I said. 'Thanks a lot.'

The door closed behind her.

'So, what do you say?' asked Olive brightly.

'Oh, yes — er, well — thanks very much, Olive.'

What else could I have said? And I do like Olive. Though not as much as Viola.

9

Our Giddy Aunt

Sam

Our giddy aunt arrived in the middle of an evening, without warning. She is our father's sister. She usually arrives without warning which wouldn't bother us if she didn't have her children with her. She has three little girls, Daisy, aged six, Buttercup, four, and Clover, two. My mother refers to them as the Flowers of the Field. Granny calls them a handful, and she's right.

Seb opened the door to them. He had gone grumbling to answer it – he was swotting for his physics exam. But I was doing maths and had answered the previous ring when it had been Mr Murchie with a pound of haddock for our mother. She refuses to open the door to anybody. They can ring all night as far as she's concerned.

'Hello, Sebastian, how *are* you?'

On hearing the voice in the hall, my mother and I lifted our heads and looked at one another.

'Sounds like Clementina,' said my mother uneasily.

The next moment Clementina had come rushing into the room, her fair hair streaming behind her (she always looks as if she's out in a force eight gale which she often is in Orkney, where she lives), and said, 'Lend me the taxi fare, be a darling, Isabella.'

Isabella had little more than the taxi fare in the house

but she gave it to her, anyway. She didn't have much choice. The taxi was standing down in the street with its engine running and the Flowers of the Field were making such a din on the back seat that one or two people had started to collect on the pavement.

'Come and give me a hand with the luggage, Samantha, would you, sweetie? And you, too, Sebastian, if you wouldn't mind.'

We trailed down the stairs after her, with Sebastian muttering about peace and families and exams. Our giddy aunt opened up the back door of the taxi and out fell the Flowers of the Field, looking somewhat bedraggled and wilted after a twelve hour journey by boat and train from Orkney. The rest of the taxi was piled high with luggage: cases and holdalls and cardboard boxes tied with string and over-full plastic bags. The taxi driver threw it all out to us hastily, and, I couldn't help thinking, gratefully. He drove off at speed down our narrow street, just avoiding scraping the side of the Quinns' blue Cortina. Their pride and joy. They both spend hours washing and polishing it.

'Need potty,' said Clover and immdiately a pool of water appeared on the pavement between her feet. Daisy and Buttercup were fighting for possession of a toy tractor. They were locked in combat like those Japanese wrestlers you see on the telly; and they had hold of each other's hair and they were screaming. Clementina sighed and ran her fingers through her long blond tresses. She's very beautiful. When I was small I used to think she was a princess. A princess that had just come out of the sea.

'Can we give you a hand?' said Mrs Quinn. She and her husband had been in the pub, were coming home.

'How kind of you,' said Clementina, giving them an

angelic smile. Mr Quinn picked up the heaviest-looking suitcase.

With a struggle we managed to get everything up the stairs and into the flat, including the Flowers, who had calmed down with the promise of something nice for supper. Haddock? Muesli? There wasn't much else in the kitchen.

'Perhaps Samantha will get you some ice-cream,' said their mother. 'If you are very, very good.'

Those three didn't know how to be good, never mind very very. Buttercup, whose hair matches her name, slid her hot, sticky hand into mine and looked up at me hopefully.

'Oh, Lord, what a journey!' said Clementina, throwing herself into a chair. 'And it was bucking like a bronco all the way across the Pentland Firth.'

'Clover pewked all over her feet,' said Daisy.

I had been wondering what the smell was.

'Have you come for a holiday, then?' asked my mother.

'Holiday nothing! I've left Donald.'

Daisy began to cry.

'She wants ice-cream,' said Buttercup.

My mother, with a look of resignation, rummaged in her purse and came up with some money.

'Take Buttercup with you, Samantha, there's a dear,' said my giddy aunt.

'I want to go too,' said Daisy.

'Me go too,' screamed Clover.

I had to take them all. Clementina said it would give her and Bella a chance to sort out the beds while we were gone. I didn't like the sound of that one bit and knew what would happen — Clementina and the children would be given my room and I would have to camp out in the living-room with my mother who sleeps on the divan. Seb has the smaller of the two bedrooms. We're tightly enough packed as it is without having four extra people dumped on us. And for how long?

We went to the chip shop for the ice-cream. As soon as the Flowers smelt the chips they started to wail afresh, so I had to buy a bag of chips and share them out.

'Salt and vinegar,' shouted Daisy.

'Salt and vinegar,' screamed Clover.

'I want sauce,' demanded Buttercup. 'Lots and lots and lots of sauce.'

After a great deal of arguing, we also bought a large tub of chocolate chip ice-cream.

'What lovely little girls,' said the man, not riled at the amount of time he was having to spend hanging over the cold cabinet. But then he's Italian and Italians are supposed to be nutty about children. Unlike me.

I walked back home with the three of them clinging to me like trailing vines. They kept trying to push up the lid of the ice-cream and dig their fingers in. I'd have to get Morag along to lend a hand. She loves children, so she says. Though she might change her mind after a few sessions with this lot.

When the ice-cream tub had been licked clean, the Flowers were led off to be bathed and put to bed. They went docilely now, utterly exhausted.

Seb had retired to his room and locked the door. My mother and I were on our own for a few minutes.

'How long are they going to stay?' I demanded.

'How do I know? And don't go on at me! You sound like your grandmother when you do. It's not my fault that they're here.'

'They can go and stay with Torquil. He's her brother, after all.'

'Don't be ridiculous! Have you seen his flat?'

87

'Why has she left Donald, anyway?'

'They had a row.' My mother shrugged, as if the cause did not interest her. 'Donald can be difficult. Locked up in his painting all the time. Of course, Clementina's not particularly easy to live with, either.'

She could say that again! I was coming to the conclusion that no one is easy to live with. Donald (nice name, Donald, says my granny — I won't need to tell you what she thinks of Clementina) is a painter and they live on an old croft on Orkney. Clementina designs and knits sweaters, fantastic ones. Neither of them makes much money.

The telephone rang and when I lifted the receiver I heard the bleeps of a pay phone.

'Is that you, Bella?'

'No, it's Sam.'

'This is Donald here.' They don't have a phone at the croft. Donald is against the intrusion of the outside world. 'Is Clementina there?'

'Yes, she is. Do you want to—'

'That's all I want to know.' He hung up.

'Donald's a single-minded man,' said my mother. 'He's probably in the middle of executing some deathless masterpiece.'

'What do people like that have to get married for?' I said irritably. I felt irritable at the thought of the uncomfortable night I would have to spend with my legs hanging over the end of the sofa. Mrs Quinn had kindly lent us some extra blankets and pillows. 'I think I'll ask Morag if I can stay with her while they're here.'

'No, don't do that, Samantha. I need you here.'

We didn't get to bed until one. Clementina, now that the Flowers were comatose, wanted to unwind, as she put it, and to talk. She gave us a picture of life on the croft which made me feel glad I lived on a city street. 'It's beautiful and wild,' she said, 'and full of magic, but sometimes I just want people.'

My mother and I got three small people around 6 a.m. without wanting them. Clover landed on my tummy and stayed there, peering into my face, trying to lift up my eyelashes. Daisy and Buttercup attempted to pull the bedclothes off my mother. She resisted. She told them to go and see their own mother. That had no effect at all.

'Mummy's sleeping,' said Daisy with finality.

'So am I.'

'No, you're not,' said Buttercup. 'I can see your eyes.'

My mother promptly closed them.

I was forced to rise and give the Flowers cocoa and biscuits, after which Daisy and Buttercup amused themselves by crayoning on old newspapers and I read to Clover from the sack of books she dragged out of the bedroom. I read about Spot the dog and Pat the Postman and busy bees and magic spiders until I was hoarse. By eight o'clock I was ready to go back to bed, except that I had no bed to go to.

My mother was up by now, unable to conceal herself under the bedclothes any longer. Buttercup and Clover had finally dragged them off her. There was still no sign of Clementina.

'Mummy sleeping,' said Clover.

'Samantha, why don't you go along the street and meet your grandmother?' suggested my mother. Head her off, she meant.

I was glad to get out into the street for a bit of peace and quiet. The sound of the traffic was like a lullaby after the screechings of the Flowers of the Field. I waved to Mr Quinn as he set off for work in his blue Cortina.

89

There was no sign of life at the numerous second-hand and antique shops. They don't open their doors up before ten, some not till midday. This is not an early morning street. The basement café was open, though; a few workmen were going in for breakfast.

When I saw Granny coming, I dashed along to meet her.

'You're up and about early today, hen.'

I told her why.

'Help my kilt!' she said. (That's one of her sayings. She doesn't actually own a kilt.) 'That's all we need! And where does Isabel think she's going to get the money from to feed them? She needn't bother looking in my direction. I'm fair skint after my holiday. Why doesn't your father do something about them?'

Torquil was in the flat when I got home from the paper round in the afternoon. The grapevine had obviously sent the news along. He was playing 'Ride a Cock Horse' and 'This Little Piggy went to Market' and 'Round and Round the Garden' with the two younger children and chatting away in betweentimes with Daisy. They were all laughing. Torquil's good with small children. I remembered him playing with Seb and me and I got a funny kind of lump in my throat. Damn him! I thought. Why couldn't he stay away and leave us in peace?

After they had been with us for a week, during which there had been no further word from Donald, our giddy aunt announced that she had got herself a job.

'A *job*?' said my mother.

'A *job*?' said my grandmother.

We were all there, sitting round the table, including the Flowers and Torquil. He had been coming every day, as had Granny. There's something about Clementina that draws people. (As there is about our mother, of course.)

'Yes, I start this evening,' said Clementina. I had thought she looked very dressed up. She was wearing a greenish-blue georgette dress (from the shop), with lots of greenish-blue eye make-up, and she had put flowers in her hair. 'In the pub on the corner. Eight till two.'

'Eight till two,' repeated my mother and looked at the Flowers who were taking drinks of red wine from everybody's glass when they weren't looking. Torquil had brought the wine. Given to him by a pal, he'd said, which had made Granny humph.

'It doesn't shut till one. And then we have to clear up. I'm sure the girls will be no bother, will you, loves?'

I thought I heard Granny mutter something about a slate loose.

The girls crowed with laughter and Clover tried to climb on to the table. As she did, she knocked over a glass of wine which went streaking across the table on to Granny's lap. She was wearing her beige-coloured trouser suit. She leapt sky-high into the air. There was a nasty-looking stain on the jacket.

'Soak it in cold water,' cried Clementina. 'Run quickly!'

'Red wine stains like nobody's business,' said Granny grimly. She took herself off to the bathroom, without deigning to hurry.

'Now listen, Clementina,' said my mother, 'I cannot promise to be in every night to look after the girls. I've already told Maudie I'd see her this evening.'

'And we've got work—' Seb and I said simultaneously.

'I'll oblige, sister dear,' said Torquil, 'especially if you could see your way to obliging me with just a little bit of the lolly. It would be for services rendered.'

'You're not going to stay here till two o'clock every morning,' said Bella.

'They'll be asleep long before two,' said Clementina. 'Won't you, petals?'

The Flowers weren't so silly that they would say yes to that. They began banging on the table with spoons and demanding ice-cream. They had seen Granny bring in a block of Neapolitan.

'Goodness me, is that the time?' cried Clementina. 'I'll have to fly.'

And she more or less did. Her feet scarcely seemed to touch the ground. She was gone before Granny returned from the bathroom looking somewhat damp all down her front.

Torquil refilled her glass. 'Drink that up, Ma. It'll make you feel better.'

'We want ice-cream,' sang Buttercup and Daisy.

'Ice-cream, ice-cream,' chanted Clover, and rocked to and fro on her chair until it threatened to topple over.

'Better fetch it, Sebastian,' said Bella with resignation.

As soon as he came back they swooped down on the ice-cream block, whooping like Red Indians.

'That's enough!' said my mother sharply, but they paid no attention. They continued to wrestle for possession.

'Give it to me *this minute!*' said Granny. 'Or none of you'll get any of it. It'll be straight to bed instead!'

They stopped and looked at her.

'I mean it,' she said and put out her hand for the block. Buttercup passed it over.

After they'd eaten their ice-cream, Granny tried to get them to go to bed and to sleep but didn't do as well there. They put on their nighties but they wouldn't stay in bed. They kept coming through for drinks of water or to say they felt sick. Clover went in and out of the bathroom every five minutes and flushed the loo.

'It would take a rubber hammer to send them to sleep,' said Seb.

'A smack on the bottom might help,' said Granny.

'We're not allowed to be smacked,' said Daisy and stuck the tip of her tongue out. 'Yah, yah, yah!' she cried and ran for the bathroom, where she locked herself in.

Clover had come back and was busy scribbling on my maths book with a purple wax crayon. I removed both the book and the crayon from her and she screamed so loudly that it was a wonder the noise didn't carry as far as the pub on the corner. But our giddy aunt, if she heard, did not appear. No doubt she was being a big success and somebody else would be pulling the pints while she leant on the bar and related the story of her life.

'This can't go on, Isabel,' said Granny.

'I know!' said Isabel wearily. We all felt weary. 'But how can I put them out on the street?'

'I think I'll be on my way, then,' said Torquil. He kissed the Flowers goodbye and shaking them off his coat tails, departed, whistling.

'I bet I know where he's going,' said Granny. 'To the pub. For a free drink. Isabel, how on earth did you ever get mixed up with a family like that, would you tell me?'

They began on the usual arguments. The Flowers were all in the bathroom with the door shut and were being suspiciously quiet. I heard water running but decided not to investigate. Instead, I made my escape and went out on to the street. I'd finished my exams that day and was feeling sort of summer holidayish. The sun was still shining on the rooftops and the sky was blue. I like long summer evenings.

I decided to go and see if Morag was in. On my way

93

along the street I saw someone familiar-looking come round the corner. He was big and burly and had a long black beard. It was Donald! I ran to meet him.

'Hi, Sam, how're you doing lass? I've come to take Clementina home. I've finished the big painting I was working on.'

'She'll never go.'

'Oh, I think she will.'

And she did, just like that, or at least, the next morning. The girls were missing their father, she said. They hung around his neck like big fat daisies. We helped pack up the bags and boxes and squeezed them into a taxi. We waved them off, Mother and Seb and I, and Granny.

As the taxi gathered speed, Clover put her head out of one window and blew us a string of kisses, and our giddy aunt put her head out of the other and called, 'Thanks for everything. Come and visit us in Orkney. You too, Mrs McKetterick!'

'That'll be the day,' said Granny.

The taxi turned the corner into the main road and was gone. I even felt a little bit sorry. The flat was going to seem awfully quiet for a day or two and I'd miss Clover.

'What a bunch!' Granny turned to Seb and me. 'One thing you two should be grateful for, at least, is that you take after me and not any of your other relatives.'

Neither Seb nor I could find an answer to that. Our mother smiled.

10

Our Ancestral Home

Seb

Every summer we go to spend a week in the home of our ancestors. Our father's ancestors. On our mother's side they don't seem to go any further back than our grandmother's grandparents. She can remember her grandfather, who was a fisherman in the nearby port of Newhaven, and her granny, who was a fisher wifie and went about in a striped skirt with a creel basket over her arm calling out, 'Haddies for sale, come buy our fresh haddies!' Or words to that effect.

Torquil's ancestors aren't at all like that. They've never done a decent day's work in their lives, as far as we can tell. Layabouts all of them, says our granny. They've lived in the castle in Argyll since Domesday, or thereabouts. Domesday just about sums them up, says our granny. The castle sits right on the edge of a promontory jutting out into the Atlantic Ocean. Next stop America. It's all very romantic when the sun's setting on a clear evening and our grandfather's promenading along the parapet walk fifty feet up wearing a kilt and playing the bagpipes. But it's not quite so romantic when it's misting or raining and you can't see further than your hand. (Sam says it's even more romantic then as that's the time that the ghosts of our ancestors are out and about!) The rainfall in Argyll is one of the highest in Scotland. Usually, when we're there, it rains.

This year was no exception.

Grandfather came to collect us in his ancient Bentley. And I mean ancient. We reckon he must bribe the local garage to get it through its M.O.T., though with what we can't imagine, since he's not exactly rolling in money. Any more than his son is.

'The whole family's batty,' says our granny. 'You can't get away from it.'

Nevertheless, she was coming with us. She doesn't like missing out on anything. 'A castle's a castle, when all's said and done.'

Our mother was coming, too. And Torquil had wanted to join us but had been dissuaded. 'It's not on,' Bella had told him flatly. 'Especially with Mother coming.'

Grandfather was late collecting us, which was only what we expected. He never has come on time, yet there we were with our bags packed, going to the window every ten minutes to look down into the street.

'Talk about unreliable!' Our grandmother humphed. He was three hours late. Every half-hour she had declared that she wasn't going to sit here like a dummy awaiting his pleasure and she was going straight home to unpack her case. She hadn't moved. 'Who does he think he is, anyway?'

And then he arrived. We heard the commotion in the street before he got as far as ringing the bell. He had double-parked and if you knew our street (it's one-way) then you'd realise what a kerfuffle that would cause. No other vehicle could get past. All they could do was honk their horns.

'Come on!' cried Bella and we grabbed our bags.

We opened the door to find Grandfather standing on

the mat, smiling, one arm raised ready to ring the bell.

'Sorry, Isabella! How lovely you're looking! Sorry, Mrs McKetterick! So nice to see you, dear lady. How you two have grown! (This was to Sam and me.) I got unaccountably delayed—'

The tempo of the horns was hotting up. We tumbled down the stairs and into the Bentley. The street was totally jammed up and there was much cursing and swearing going on.

Grandpa invited our grandmother to sit in the front beside him. He held the door open and bowed and she stepped in, a bit like the Queen Mother. A bit.

'It might be old,' she said, patting the leather seat, 'but it's got class. Good things never wear out, say what you like.'

Grandfather gave a last wave to the line of cars behind him and got into the driver's seat, taking his time like he always does. The car started first time. At least that was something. (It doesn't always.) We were off!

For the first two hours we bowled smoothly along, heading westward and northward.

'Yes, it's a grand old car,' said Grandfather, patting the steering wheel lovingly, and as if on cue the engine immediately began to splutter, to show that it shouldn't be taken for granted. It spluttered some more, gave a final hiccupping cough, and died. Miles from anywhere, of course. Miles from a garage, certainly.

Our grandmother sucked in her breath and clutched her handbag firmly to her chest. Bella sat back with resignation. Sam, Grandfather and I got out to inspect the engine. He lifted up the bonnet and we gazed into its innards. They looked as if they could be doing with a good clean.

'Well, what do you think, Sebastian old man?'

Since I'm not a trained motor mechanic there was not a lot I could think. Grandfather moved one or two wires around and decided to give the engine another go. Nothing happened.

'What about petrol?' suggested Bella.

'Petrol! You might just be on to something there, Isabella! The gauge is broken, you see, so it's difficult to tell.'

'When did you last put any in?'

'Now let me see. . . .' He could not quite remember. 'Last week . . . perhaps? Bless me, I think we must be out of petrol.' He did have an empty can in the boot and you can probably guess who got the job of going back to the nearest garage.

'It's miles,' said Sam.

'You're young, both of you. You've got winged feet! You'll be there and back in no time.' He slid his hand into his pocket and brought it out again, empty. 'I don't suppose either of you ladies would have a fiver to spare?'

'No different from his son, not one whit!' said Granny under her breath as she handed one over.

We grumbled about our relatives as we slogged the three miles — winged feet indeed! — back to the garage, wondering how we had come to have such a crazy collection.

'Morag's father or grandfather would never run out of petrol,' said Sam.

'Neither would Hari's,' said I. Nor Viola's either. The very idea was unthinkable. It would be just my luck if she and her parents were to come along now and sweep past us in their brand-new, faultless car. Although, I wouldn't have minded a glimpse of her. Since that Saturday when she'd come into the shop I had a feeling she was avoiding me.

'What are you thinking about?' asked Sam. 'It's all right — don't tell me! You really are love-sick, aren't you?'

'What about yourself?' She and Morag had been playing a lot of tennis with two boys in their class at school. She blushed and stuck her tongue out at me.

By the time we got back to the car our two female relatives were growing restless.

'I was beginning to think we were going to be stuck here all day,' said Granny. 'It'll be dark by the time we get to the castle.'

'It's light till late in summer,' said Grandfather with a smile. He is never restless, never in a hurry, never bad-tempered.

He poured the petrol in; the car purred into life.

'Capital!' he declared. 'Just what the doctor ordered.'

'We'd better get some more at the next garage,' said Bella, who, in the face of her father-in-law, becomes amazingly practical. 'We don't want to get caught short again.'

Granny produced a tenner for the next batch and said she'd be skint before she ever got started on her holiday. She also said her stomach thought her throat had been cut and if she didn't have something to eat soon she'd pass out. We stopped at a roadside café where she treated us to tea and scones. The scones bounced as they hit the plates.

'I'll make you some proper scones,' Granny promised Grandfather. 'As light as a feather they'll be.'

So, with all this stopping and starting, it was quite late when we reached our ancestral home. It stood lonely and dramatic-looking against the darkening sky and it did give me quite a thrill just to see it there, as did the sound of the sea washing against the rocks. There is something very special about the west coast. The air is soft and balmy and the hills are blue. It's a mystical place, says Bella, who claims she wouldn't mind living there. Except that she'd miss the street.

The castle is an ancient stone fortified house, tall and narrow, with a gabled roof and slits for windows, marvellous for firing arrows out of, not so good for letting in light. There are also numerous shot-holes which let in the sea breezes. An internal spiral stone staircase winds dizzyingly round and round, with steps so worn that you have to tread carefully and keep one hand on the rail and the other on the wall. The castle's outer walls are three metres thick. Even in summer the air inside is chill.

Granny shivered.

'I told you you should have brought your winter coat,' said Bella, who was wrapped in a long green mohair cloak looking like Deirdre of the Sorrows — so Sam said. I don't know who this Deirdre was but she sounded a bit like Bella. Not that our mother is ever drowned too deep in sorrow.

We had beans on toast for supper. The toast had to be made from sliced white bread which made Deirdre wrinkle her nose with distaste. Tomorrow, she said, she would bake some bread. She had forgotten about the state of bread in this part of Argyll. Our grandfather bought it from a van that called once a week. And, by the way, I should have told you that we have no grandmother on our father's side — she died before we were born. 'Poor woman,' is the verdict of our very-much-alive grandmother. 'I don't suppose she fancied lingering long in this life.'

I slept in a little turret room which had just enough room for a single bed. From its window I could look

100

across the ocean. The bed was damp so I slept in my dry sleeping bag which I had brought with me. I was well prepared, having suffered before.

I don't know whether I was awakened by the drumming of the rain or the loud hallooing of Grandfather up the stairs, but waken I did, to hear both the rain and Grandfather. 'Give us a hand, Sebastian old man, there's a good chap,' he was calling. I crawled out of the bag and pulled on a sweater and jeans. I heard Sam's voice on the floor below. It was pitch black on the other side of my long narrow window, and raining heavily.

We were being summoned for drip drill. We had to creep around in the roof space while Grandfather held a torch, and arrange the vast array of buckets and bowls in the right places. Drips hit us in the eye and plonked on the tops of our heads.

'Regular old colander, isn't it?' said Grandfather cheerfully.

At that point the torch went out, leaving Sam and me in total blackness. She screamed and clutched my arm. I didn't feel too jolly myself. I had never known such utter blackness.

'Hang on,' called Grandfather. 'I'll just go and get a new battery.'

'He won't have a new battery,' said Sam.

We held on to one another, unable to move, listening to the loud tattoo of the rain over our heads.

Grandfather didn't have a battery; he came back with a box of matches which he struck one by one until we managed to manoeuvre our way across the attic floor round the rapidly filling receptacles to the hatch. Then we dropped down onto the relatively safe and dry floor. Granny was standing there, with the cord firmly knotted round her woolly dressing gown and her hands on her hips.

'Look at the two of you! You're like drookit hens! You'll catch your death if you don't get out of those wet things at once.'

None of us got up too early in the morning. In fact, it was lunchtime by the time we surfaced, which didn't really matter as the rain had gone, to be replaced by a fine mist of the kind which drapes itself like a cloak round you as soon as you set a foot outside. It came down as far as our ankles.

'Not much to see, is there,' said Granny, poking her nose outside. 'It looks like I'm going to get on with my knitting this week. I hope the telly's working.'

It was, though only after a fashion, and it was black and white. It wasn't the same, said Granny, watching *Dynasty* and *Dallas* robbed of their colour; and every now and then a snowstorm obliterated those glittering people entirely.

In spite of the mist and rain Sam and I spent a lot of time outside. We pulled up the worst of the weeds in the garden and we walked for miles, exploring our old haunts up the coast. The rain had a special soft west-coast feel to it; it was quiet rain, and, falling on the leaves, it whispered rather than pattered. The whole world seemed quiet. And the mist shrouded the caravans in the field behind the castle garden. We had been very upset when Grandfather had had to sell that field. We used to play football and Cowboys and Indians in it when we were younger and we were particularly fond of a huge copper beech tree in the middle.

'The old place could do with a bit of renovation,' I said. We were standing in the driveway surveying the ancestral home.

'I wonder how Viola would fancy a castle?' said Sam. 'She'd probably want something plushy, like a split-level bungalow, furnished by Liberty.'

I gave Sam a shove and sent her off balance. As she was recovering she glanced behind her. 'Who's that?' she said.

I turned to look. A figure was looming up out of the mist. A man's figure. It raised its arm in salutation. We waited and as it drew closer it became disturbingly familiar.

'I think it might be Torquil,' said Sam in a strangled-sounding voice.

We both felt strangled and unable to speak when we saw that there was no possibility of it being anyone other than our father. There would be the devil to pay when our female relatives saw him. He addressed us heartily.

'Greetings, Offspring! How goes it here?' Positioning himself between us and draping an arm round each of our shoulders, he propelled us towards the massive, studded door of the castle. He pushed it open with his toe and called out, 'Anyone at home?' His voice echoed up the spiral staircase but was not heard, for the rest of the family was in the kitchen huddled round the Aga cooker.

Our grandmother had been making dropped scones. (Small, thick pancakes, to Sassenachs, and if you don't know what a Sassenach is then look it up in the dictionary!) On seeing Torquil, she dropped the scones flat on the stone-flagged floor, which hadn't been washed for months.

'Help my kilt!' she said, staring at our father. 'This is all we need.'

'How did you get here?' asked Bella.

'I hitched. I'm on my way to visit my old pal Hector in Skye so I thought I'd drop off and say hello.'

'Hello,' said Bella. 'And goodbye.'

'Come now, Isabella....'

Grandfather came forward to clap his son on the back. 'Stay the night, old son.' He looked appealingly at Bella. I thought for a moment he was going to ask them to join hands and make up. 'I'm sure there's plenty of room for everybody.'

'Not when there's only one warm place to sit in there isn't,' muttered Granny, supposedly in an aside, but perfectly audibly.

Torquil smiled at her and produced a bottle wrapped in brown paper from his pocket. 'I have a present for you, Ma.' It was port, her favourite tipple.

She consented to have a glass. She sat by the stove and propped her feet on an old orange crate. We saw her mellow visibly, like a flower which has been clamped shut unfolds when the sun comes out. Bella, too, sipped a glass. Sam and I drank hot chocolate and ate pineapple upside-down-cake which our mother had made and not dropped on the floor.

'It's nice to have the family together,' said Grandfather. 'Pity Clementina and Donald and the girls couldn't have been here, too.'

Granny's eyes goggled at the thought.

Torquil stayed for three days. He rose early every morning and hauled Sam and me out of our beds.

'What's got into you?' said Granny.

'It's the country air, Mother-in-law!'

He and Sam and I went fishing in a nearby loch and we rowed the old boat round the coast to watch the seabirds and when the mist lifted and the sun came out we swam in the brilliantly clear, green sea and afterwards lay on a white sandy lick of beach.

'Reminds me of when I was a boy,' said Torquil, with his arms pillowed behind his head and his eyes on the sky.

In the evenings we played Monopoly and Cluedo and Scrabble and Murder. The castle was good for Murder. Even Granny joined in and went round the spiral staircase looking for hidey-holes, of which there were many. And she screamed with the rest of us. Sam and I managed to murder one another and Torquil murdered Granny and Bella murdered Torquil. The screams echoing throughout the castle caused a man to come running up from one of the caravans.

'It's all right,' Grandfather told the man cheerfully. 'We're just murdering one another.'

On the morning that Torquil left, Sam and I walked with him to the main road. He was looking younger and fitter than he had done for a long time.

'It's been great fun,' he said. 'I came because I wanted to see a bit more of you two.'

A lorry came round the corner. He stuck out his thumb. It stopped.

'Cheers, Offspring! Take care!'

He swung himself up into the cab and the lorry took off. We waved until it was out of sight.

We felt quiet going home. Bella was in a tetchy mood in the kitchen. She was cutting up onions for soup and they were flying in all directions.

'Just as well he didn't stay any longer,' said Granny, who was reading a three-week-old copy of the *Oban Times*.

'Why do you have to say that?' snapped Bella. 'You enjoyed his company — you can't deny it!'

'Don't tell me you're going soft on him again!'

'Don't be ridiculous!'

We left them to it. Sam went upstairs to finish writing a letter to Morag. I went back outside and found Grandfather cutting a cabbage in the vegetable garden. It looked a bit slug-infested.

'There'll be nothing the matter with it once we've cut the holes out,' he said. 'No chemicals have touched it, that's the main thing.'

We moved round the garden looking at the beans and carrots and the straggly rows of potatoes. Once, Grandfather had had a gardener who worked full time. The flowers in the flower garden were half choked with weeds; Sam and I had not made much impression on them.

'You'll need to come back again and stay longer next time, Sebastian.'

We strolled around the policies, as Grandfather calls them, which took no more than fifteen or twenty minutes. Not so very long ago the family had owned all the land round about. The caravan field had been the last to go. There was nothing left to sell off now, except the garden.

'We'll never let that go, Sebastian. Imagine, caravans right up to the front door!'

We inspected the crumbling dry-stone dyke which separated the caravan field from the garden, and gazed up at the castle walls which badly needed repointing. Fortunately, from where we stood we couldn't see the roof.

'Old place could do with a touch up here and there. Nothing that someone young and strong couldn't cope with.'

Someone with half a million in the bank.

'One of these days, Sebastian,' said Grandfather, waving his hand in the air, 'it'll all be yours.

11

Family Fortunes

Sam

'Children, I think we're going to have to sell the shop,' said our mother. When she calls us children, we know it's serious.

We were sitting round the table and we had just finished supper. Bella had started by saying she had something to tell us, something she had been turning over and over in her head for days. We had noticed she'd been preoccupied and Seb had said to me, 'What's up with Bella?' and I'd shrugged. She'd been a bit unsettled ever since we'd come back from our trip to Argyll. Ever since Torquil had turned up there. I'd had the feeling that that might be at the back of it.

But it seemed I was wrong.

'I mean it,' she said, for we were staring at her with disbelief.

'You can't sell!' I protested. I couldn't imagine life without the shop. Without the silks and satins and crêpe de Chines, without the excitement of new stock coming in. And I'd miss the cosiness of it when folk came in and blethered and drank fennel tea.

'I don't *want* to sell — you know that — but we need the money, I'm afraid.'

'But we wouldn't get much money if we did sell it,' said Seb. 'It's heavily mortgaged, don't forget, and by the time we'd paid the legal fees—'

'Prices have gone up though in the street since we bought.'

In fact, the street is undergoing quite a renovation. It's coming up in the world! I hope it will never come too far up, I like it the way it is, with its mix of folk and shops. People are getting grants to clean the old stone of the tenements and the shops are trying to jump themselves up, become trendy. And even the café which used to sell salads and carrot cake is now doing meals with the menu written in French.

'But we took out a second mortgage last year,' Seb reminded our mother, 'to pay for our share of the roof bill. We don't actually own much of it.'

Bella sighed. 'I hate money.'

'That's not true.' Seb always has to be very precise. 'It's not money you hate but—'

'All right, I know – it's lack of it! Anyway, I still think we're going to have to sell.'

'But why. Why just now?'

'The rates are due next month. For the flat as well as the shop.'

So that was it! And the rates in Edinburgh had gone up drastically. Everyone was moaning, from the man who owned Granny's supermarket to the Quinns next door.

Seb was still not going to let our mother off the hook. He was frowning. I really think he should become some sort of investigator when he grows up. He said, 'Bella, what do you *mean* – the rates are due next month? You've been paying them monthly by banker's order, haven't you? *Haven't* you?'

Well, she hadn't. We could see that by the look on

her face so Seb hadn't really needed to ask a second time.

'So now we've got to find the rates for a *whole* year in one go?'

'Sebastian, stop going on at me! I've only been trying to do my best.'

'Did you *cancel* the banker's orders?'

'Yes, I did.' She tossed her head crossly. 'And I did it because we were having a job to manage every month.'

'That's great, isn't it? So how are we going to manage every year?'

'I won't be spoken to in that tone of voice!' She got up and began to gather up the plates, clattering and banging them together. I was annoyed with Seb. He goes too far with her at times.

'It's all right, Mother. There's always Granny — she's got a wee bit tucked away. I expect we'll manage. We usually do.'

'This is different, Samantha,' she said in a low voice.

'You're telling me it is,' said Seb. 'We must be talking about something over a thousand pounds.'

That silenced me. For the first time I began to realise it really was serious and that we might have to sell the shop.

We were clearing up, still in silence, when we heard the flat door opening.

'That'll be your grandmother,' said Bella. 'Not a word to her — not yet anyway, until we know what we're going to do.'

'But she might be able to lend us a hundred or two,' I objected.

'Anyone in?'

The moment Granny entered the room we saw there

109

was something up. She usually comes in purposefully as if she's got no time to dither about. This evening her body looked kind of slack and her face was greyish. She looked older, a lot older. She sank down into an armchair with the air of somebody who never means to get out of it again.

'Are you all right, Granny?' I cried. 'Is it your ulcer?'

'No, it's not my ulcer, though it's a wonder it's not. But I'm not all right. Far from it. I've just had bad news.'

We waited, for she was not going to divulge it in one rush. What could have happened? I wondered. Had she found dry rot in her flat? Everybody who lives in old buildings lives in dread of that. Morag's flat nearly fell apart with it a year or so ago and fixing it all but bankrupted them. Or maybe Charlie the budgie had died. Or Etta might be ill with some dreadful disease.

Granny looked up at us and announced, 'I'm being made redundant. I'm to be retired, believe it or not. *Me*, at the age of sixty-two! I still feel like a young woman. I'm not ready for the scrap heap, not yet I'm not! I've got years of work left in me.' Her vigour was coming back, and the colour into her cheeks. 'He's said I can go at the end of next week, just like that! After all the years I've slaved my fingers to the bone for him. And he'll give me a month's wages as a goodbye present. Big deal! He's putting his nephew into my place, that's what he's doing. He's a right sleekit one that nephew, he's been hanging round the place for the last week or two grinning like a Cheshire cat!'

'But that's terrible, Granny,' I said. 'Especially when we're going to have to sell—'

'Sell what?'

So I'd let the cat out of the bag! Another big, grinning Cheshire one. I hadn't meant to. Bella and Seb were

110

glaring at me, but, after all, Granny would have to know sooner or later.

'Some family we are,' she said, 'We'll all be living on the buroo.' By that she meant the dole.

'I'm going to take a job,' said Bella.

'Doing what?' demanded her mother.

'Don't let's all quarrel,' I said. 'We've got to put our heads together.'

'The girl's right.' Granny glanced over at the cupboard. 'I could be doing with a wee drop of port, Isabel, if you have any.'

We spent all evening talking. We're good at talking, and, as Seb observed, if we could only get paid for that we'd be able to live in clover. (One of Granny's phrases.)

We considered turning the shop into something more lucrative than a second-hand clothes business, or at least adding another line to it. But what? We could sell hand-knitted jumpers, suggested Granny, everybody seemed to be into that nowadays. Folk were prepared to pay high prices for good hand-knitted stuff. We could get women to knit for us at home – there were plenty about with not enough to do, in her opinion; women like herself who'd been axed from jobs in their prime or who'd spent their lives bringing up kids and had never had the chance to work at all.

'I doubt if we'd make a fortune from that,' said Seb.

He's always the one who throws cold water on schemes. Just as well, he says, one of us has got to have his head screwed on.

'We're not talking about making a fortune,' said Granny. 'We're talking about staying alive.'

'But, Gran, what we need first of all is hard cash to pay the rates with.'

111

I had been doodling on a piece of paper. 'Listen!' I said. 'If we pay every woman twenty pounds to knit a sweater and sell it for fifty then we'd make a profit of thirty and we'd only need about thirty-five sweaters to clear a thousand pounds. Let's say forty. That's not all that many.'

'You're right, hen.' Granny nodded approvingly. 'I've seen jumpers they've been asking sixty and seventy for, even. I can't imagine who buys them at that price but it seems there's plenty folk about with more money than sense.'

'But we'd have to buy the wool first,' said Seb. 'And we'd also have to have the money to pay the women before we sold the sweaters. You couldn't expect them to wait. And where do you find all these women?'

'I could knit one,' I said, 'and so could Morag. We could all knit one.'

'Count me out.' Seb got up and pulled on his anorak. 'You used to knit scarves when you were little.'

'And do you really think we could sell *your* knitting?'

The last time I'd knitted a sweater the arms hadn't turned out too well, I have to admit. (They'd actually come down to my knees.) But it was typically mean of Seb to bring that up. After delivering that nasty swipe, he went out to prowl the streets. He had taken to doing that. Hoping to bump into dear Viola, no doubt.

I felt restless, too. And I was peckish. I decided to go to the chip shop. Granny gave me some money and asked me to buy her a fish supper. She'd been so upset earlier that she'd felt sick to her stomach and hadn't had any tea.

It was quiet in the chip shop. I said to Albert, the man who runs it, 'I don't suppose you could use some help, could you? Evenings?'

'Do you mean you?' He shook on the salt and vinegar. I nodded.

'You're too young, love.'

We weren't getting many breaks, were we? I walked home munching my chips, looking in the windows of shops that were managing to pay their rates. But I couldn't see us going into the greengrocery business or setting up as fishmongers or bakers. I wouldn't have minded a bookshop, for then I'd have the chance to read all the new books as they came in, but it seems you don't make much money from selling books, either. Now if it were videos.... Videos? No, Bella wouldn't go for that. She says half of the video films are just cheap and nasty. We don't have a video recorder ourselves, something that Morag's mum can't get over. What do you do with yourselves? she asks.

I met Morag on the corner and told her our troubles. She and her mother are grand knitters — as well as bakers, if you recall — and she said they would both knit for us, if we liked. Her mother knits while she watches the telly and the video films so that means she gets a lot of knitting done. And we wouldn't have to pay them until we'd sold the sweaters, said Morag. They even have bagfuls of wool in the house; her mother buys it in sales like she buys most things, seldom ever paying full price. Her mother is a very organised, thrifty, far-seeing woman who would always be able to pay the rates.

'That would be great, Morag! You'd have to knit awful fast, though. The rates are due at the end of next month.'

I went home to tell my little bit of good news.

'She's a right sensible lass is Morag,' said Granny. 'It's amazing that the two of you are such good friends.'

Morag and I began a knitting craze. We knitted at lunchtime, during breaks between classes, and sometimes in classes themselves where the teachers were either short-sighted or sitting dozing at their desks, and we got a number of other girls in our year going on the needles, too. Within a week Morag had produced a fantastic red and green sweater in a diamond pattern and her mother an Aran cardigan. (I had got only half up the back of my jumper which was looking a little grubby, but then, as Morag said, it probably wasn't the wisest thing in the world to choose white wool, especially when we were doing so much knitting in the school playground and in the park while we waited for a tennis court.)

'Look!' I said, spreading our first two knitwear garments out on the counter in front of Bella.

'They're lovely, dear.'

I was annoyed by her lack of enthusiasm and said so.

'I do think they're lovely. But I still don't see how we'll get the rates together before the thirtieth of September.'

She sold both sweaters that afternoon which cheered her a bit. I went round to pay Morag and her mother for their labours and the wool and then I put the rest of the money into a box labelled **RATES**. We now had fifty-five pounds.

Granny finished work on the Saturday. We found it difficult to think that she wouldn't be standing behind the till again, ringing up sales or stacking wire baskets or overseeing her two assistants while they stocked the shelves with tins of pineapple and baked beans. She'd have no more tales to tell of the antics of the customers or how she'd managed to thwart would-be shoplifters. She'd have no more wage packets, either.

'I'll just have my pension from now on, and I won't get very fat on that.' I looked at her hips but made no comment. Sometimes I can keep my mouth shut. 'Unless I get another job, of course.' She was studying the Situations Vacant in the *Evening News*, had already applied for two or three shop jobs but been told in each case that she was too old. 'Too old!' she snorted. 'I could show those young ones a thing or two when it comes to stamina.'

'You can always knit in the meantime.'

'Aye, maybe.' She had never been too keen on knitting. 'I've got Etta on the job, though. She's not half bad. She's making a lacy bedjacket.'

'I'm not sure that that's the kind of thing that'll go in our shop, Gran.'

She humphed. 'Folk are often glad of a bed-jacket. You never know when you might get whisked into the hospital.' She herself always kept a good clean night-dress tucked away in a drawer, just in case.

Morag arrived to call for me and we went off to the tennis courts where we'd arranged to meet these two boys in our class, Rick and John. None of us is much good at tennis but we have a good laugh. We play mixed doubles. I play with Rick and Morag plays with John. Usually Rick and I beat Morag and John for Rick's got quite a good service — that means he can get the ball in the right court more often than the rest of us — and, although I say it myself, Morag might be a better knitter, but I am much better than she is at hitting the ball straight. She tends to send it flying miles out of the court.

One of her wild swipes biffed the ball right over the top of the netting and into the next court. I ran after it. Morag's ball had disrupted play on that court as well as

115

ours. It had struck one of the four girls on the face. She was nursing her cheek and her partner was hovering around, asking if she was all right.

'I'm awfully sorry,' I began and as the injured girl removed her hand, I saw that it was the light of Seb's life.

'Oh, it's you, Samantha,' she said and smiled, even though her face looked as if it had taken quite a wallop.

'I didn't hit it—'

'It's all right, no harm done. How's Sebastian?'

The other girl moved over to the net, leaving Viola and me standing on the sidelines together.

'Fine. Well, not really. He's worried. We all are. You see, we're having a bit of trouble at the moment.' And before I knew it I had launched into the Tale of the Rates. I knew, though, that if Seb could have heard me he'd have killed me.

The other girls were getting restless. 'Are you coming, Viola?' called one.

I picked up my ball, which I noticed looked bald compared to the fluffy ones Viola's friends were batting up and down with their rackets, and made to go.

'Tell Sebastian I was asking for him,' Viola shouted after me.

'I thought you were going to stay over there all night,' said Morag.

I almost stuck my tongue out at her but thought better of it. (If we'd been on our own, I would have done.)

Rick and I changed ends with Morag and John.

'By the way,' said Rick, 'I was telling my mother about your knitting business and she says she'll knit for you if you want. She's a reall snazzy knitter. She made my red and black sweater.'

'Marvellous!'

It was my turn to serve. I got every one of my serves in, first time.

By the twenty-third of September we had collected three hundred and ten pounds towards the rates.

'We'll never make it,' said Seb. 'Not unless a miracle occurs.'

'Or everyone knits like blazes,' said Granny. She had still had no luck over a job. She spent a good part of each day trudging round the newsagents, reading the ads sellotaped to their windows.

Even I could see that we were not going to make it on the sale of our sweaters, and as for a miracle ... I sighed.

'You've done very well with the sweaters, Samantha,' said my mother. 'Really well.'

'But not well enough.'

'No one could expect to build up a new business line in a month.' Bella looked at Seb. 'Oh – while I remember, Sebastian – a friend of yours was in yesterday. She bought that nice jersey in different shades of green that Rick's mother knitted. She'd got money for her birthday. She sent her regards. Pretty girl. Her name was Viola.'

'That reminds me! I saw her at the tennis courts the other night and she was asking for you.'

Seb leapt about three feet into the air. 'Why does no one ever tell me these things?' he demanded.

'Calm down,' I said. 'And it's too late now to go mooching round her street. Her father might think you were loitering and call the police.'

I ducked, and at that moment the doorbell rang.

'I don't feel like company,' said Bella, as I went to open the door.

'Unless it's got a thousand pounds in its pocket,' I said.

I opened the door to my father. He was wearing a new corduroy suit in a soft shade of blue. He was smiling.

'Hello, Samantha love.' He kissed me. He had recently shaved.

'I don't know whether Mother—'

'I rather think she'll be pleased to see me.'

He actually did have a thousand pounds, and more, in his pocket! He'd been doing competitions – has been doing them for years – and had won a car. We couldn't believe it. He was talking about it as calmly as if he won competitions every week.

'You could have the car or take the money. So I took the money.'

'How much?' asked Granny.

'Seven thousand.'

'Seven thousand,' repeated Granny faintly. 'Oh, my giddy aunt!'

I thought she was going to swoon. I felt kind of funny myself and had to shake my head to make sure I was hearing correctly.

'Come off it, Torquil!' said our mother. 'You're having us on.'

But he wasn't. And he was giving us the money to pay the year's rates on both the flat and the shop and, in addition, he handed over a hundred each to Seb and me, to spend on whatever we liked, and a hundred to Granny, too. To Bella, he gave five hundred.

We all hugged and kissed him, even our grandmother, who is not known for displaying affection towards our father. I'd only ever seen her giving him a peck on the cheek at New Year before.

'Sit yourself down, Torquil,' she said. 'Take this chair

here.' She indicated the best one, the one she usually sits in herself, the only one with its springs intact. 'Pour the man a wee drop of port, Isabel. We've something to celebrate.'

'You're telling me,' said Bella, as she did what she was told. 'I still can't believe it. A miracle *has* happened.'

'It seems like our luck has changed right enough,' said Granny.

12

Riches

Seb

So, we were in the money! We could hardly believe it. We kept examining our ten pound notes and holding them up to the light. I have to admit that for a few minutes I did wonder whether Torquil might not have manufactured them himself and be having us on. But they were real all right.

'What are you going to spend your money on then, Sebastian?' asked Torquil.

'I'll need to think about it,' I said, though I already had, and was almost sure I would buy a new bicycle or, at least, a new second-hand one. My old bike was falling to pieces. When Hari and I went out together he had to keep waiting for me at the tops of hills.

'And you, Samantha?' Our father turned to her.

She had a whole string of things in mind. Pink shoes, a denim jacket, a dozen records, coloured stationery, books, trainers, tennis shorts, a tennis racket, six new tennis balls—'

'You're awfully keen on tennis all of a sudden,' I said.

She ignored my remark and continued, 'A track suit—'

'Your hundred pounds'll need to be elastic,' said our grandmother.

'Have you any idea what a good tennis racket will cost?' I asked.

'I shall make out a list. And then choose,' she added rather sadly, for I suppose she'd had a vision of all those things spread out in front of her.

'And you, Isabella?' asked Torquil.

'Oh, I shall need time to think! But I have a notion to buy a *new* dress. I haven't had one for years, not brand-new. And maybe even a coat. And I shall go into a bookshop and buy anything I fancy.'

Now it was Granny's turn.

'I'm saving mine for a rainy day. With a family like this you can always be sure there'll be plenty of down-pours up ahead.'

There was one question we were all dying to ask. It was Granny who did.

'And what about you, Torquil? What are you going to spend the rest of the money on?'

'That would be telling!' he said and went on smiling.

We had to wait a week before he did tell us.

The seven days were eventful.

Grandfather, having heard of his son's good fortune, came over from Argyll and stayed a night.

'Don't forget your ancestral home, dear boy. There's a tile or two off the roof.'

'The money I've got would go nowhere on that, Father.' For once, I thought Torquil was being sensible. I wouldn't have put my money into the roof, either.

'The Bentley could be doing with a new clutch.'

'I'll pay for that.' Torquil didn't add, 'And that's all', but his tone implied it. Grandfather, probably not having hoped for as much, accepted happily, acquired a new clutch the next day and set off back for Argyll urging

121

us all to come and visit him again soon.

'I still haven't got properly warmed up since the last holiday,' said Granny, as we waved him goodbye. We turned to go back in the stair. 'The next thing'll be a visit from Clementina and company!'

But they did not arrive, though a letter for Torquil did, with an Orkney postmark on the envelope. If he could see his way to making them just a *small* loan. . . .

'I'm not sure that I'd want to win the pools,' said Granny. 'All these begging letters!'

'Clementina is not begging,' said Torquil. 'She has often enough seen me out of a tight spot. On occasions she's given me her last tenner.' He sent her fifty pounds.

'At this rate he's going to have nothing left,' said Granny.

I decided I'd better spend my hundred before Torquil asked for it back to pay his electricity bill. Hari and I went round nearly every bicycle shop in Edinburgh inspecting what was on offer, and in the end got a pretty good bargain, trading in my old heap at the same time. My new machine had ten gears, a lightweight frame, and was painted silver and red. Bella complained when I brought it into the hall.

'I'm not going to leave it downstairs chained to the railings.' Bicycle thieves came out at nights with wire cutters strong enough to break open the strongest chain.

'We're going to get an entry-phone on the stair,' said Bella. We *were* coming up in the world, along with everyone else in the street! The Quinns had been pressing for one for ages but had been having trouble in getting all the neighbours to agree to pay their share — and that had included us. 'So when we do get it installed you'll be able to leave your bike downstairs in perfect safety.'

In the meantime, the bike came indoors with me. Bella did not really mind. She was in too good a mood. She was enjoying going round the shops. And she was enjoying being taken out by Torquil, which made us a little uneasy.

Granny humphed and pursed her lips. 'I hope he doesn't think he's going to buy her back.'

He was wining and dining her, as they say (as Granny and Etta said), taking her to expensive restaurants, the theatre, the cinema, Scottish Opera, and one day he hired a car and drove her down to the Borders.

'Mother's not daft, you know.' said Sam.

Sam was having a problem with her list. When she had costed each item she realised that she couldn't have everything. The tennis gear won out. She spent hours on the courts, or hanging around them, and brought Rick home to supper one evening. Just like that. Without any fuss. She introduced him to Bella and Granny, and we all sat down to eat, and it was as if he had been coming to supper for years. They gabbed away and teased one another and when Sam got up to wash the dishes, he dried. Why couldn't it be like that for me with Viola?

I discussed the matter with Hari.

'You've got to be more forceful,' he said.

Forceful? That sort of talk wouldn't go down well in our feminist household.

'I don't mean *drag* her to the cinema. But maybe you should just walk up the path to her front door and ring the bell and ask to speak to her. Don't do it when you're delivering the papers – that puts you in an inferior position.'

It was all right for him to talk: he hadn't seen Viola's mother and father, those paragons of efficiency and the

Successful Life. However, I decided to take his advice.

I put on my new denim jacket and rode my new red and silver bicycle up to her front gate. I parked it against the fence and walked up the path, trying to look as if I wasn't at all bothered. Don't think too much, Hari had said, just do it!

Before I could hesitate, I put out my hand and pulled the brass bell. I listened to the sound of it echoing inside. After a moment, I heard footsteps. My throat felt like a dust bowl. I cleared it, got ready. *May I speak to Viola please...?* Viola herself might come to the door. If I was lucky.

The door swung inward and there stood her mother, with her spectacles dangling from a cord round her neck and a fountain pen in one hand. I had obviously disturbed her in the middle of some important business. She raised an eyebrow at me.

'May I – hum – er, speak to – er, Viola, please?' I felt such a fool and I was well aware that my face had turned brick-red.

'I'm sorry, she's not in at the moment.'

The next thing I knew I was walking back down the path. And I hadn't even asked her mother to tell Viola I'd called, or left my name. What a fool I was! I cursed inside my head, calling myself every kind of idiot that had ever walked the earth. Then I noticed that my bicycle had gone and my heart dropped somewhere into the region of my stomach.

I looked and looked again but it was *not* there. I blinked. The pavement was totally empty of bicycles of any kind. I hadn't bothered to lock mine up. I'd thought I'd only be a few minutes – and I had been – and thieves wouldn't be hanging around under the trees of a street like Viola's. But it seemed I'd been wrong. Very wrong.

124

I ran all the way home in case Sam had followed me and taken it as some sort of joke. She was quite indignant when I asked her.

'What do you take me for?' She was playing records with Rick.

Bella was not at home, being out on the town with Torquil, no doubt. I ran then to Hari's. My heart was beating like a drum by the time I got to his flat and my sweat shirt was just that. Soaked in sweat.

'You'll have to report it to the police,' said Hari at once.

'Fat lot of good that'll do!' I said, but we went anyway.

They weren't hopeful. I gave them the serial number, I'd written it down.

'You just can't leave your bikes anywhere un-padlocked, lads.'

'But it was only for a minute.'

'That's what they all say. I hope you had it insured?'

I hadn't got round to that. My previous bike hadn't been worth insuring.

Hari and I walked gloomily home.

'I'm sorry, Seb. What a break!'

What a disaster, from start to finish! My hundred pounds was blown and I didn't even have my old bike. And I still hadn't managed to make a date with Viola.

'Perhaps your father will give you another hundred?'

I wouldn't ask him.

Next day Granny brought her hundred round. She laid the ten ten pound notes on the table in front of me, like a fan.

'I told you I was keeping it for a rainy day, didn't I? Well, it seems to me it's fair pouring at the moment.'

In the end, Bella gave me fifty and I accepted fifty from

Granny. I didn't really feel it was fair to take any of her money when she'd lost her job but she insisted.

'I wouldn't give it to you if I didn't want to, would I now? You know me well enough.'

Hari and I did a repeat performance round the bicycle shops and I actually ended up with a slightly better bike than the last one. It was green and silver. Bella arranged the insurance on it straight away. I rode around the town on my new bike feeling pretty good and, yes, I did take a few turns down Viola's street, without seeing Viola. Everyone else seemed to see her. Hari caught sight of her going down the main road and they waved to one another but he couldn't think of an excuse to cross the road and start up a conversation. Sam met her on her paper round, and at the tennis courts. I went down to the courts a few times. She didn't turn up those evenings, needless to say. Granny often talks about things 'not being meant'. I had a horrible feeling that Viola and I were not 'meant' to get together.

'Had a girl in here not long ago,' said Etta, when I went to hand my bag in. 'She was asking after you. Nice lass. Very pretty. She was in paying their papers.'

'Did she have dark hair and brown eyes?'

'She did.'

'How long ago?'

'Oh, no more than ten or fifteen minutes.'

I raced out of the shop and leapt on to my machine. I caught up with Viola just before she turned the corner into her street. She was walking slowly.

'Hi!' I said, trying to sound surprised. (I'm not very good at all this play-acting but then you already know that.)

'Hello, Sebastian.' She smiled.

I got off the bike and stood with one foot in the road

and the other on the edge of the kerb. I faced her. *Ask her! Go on, ask her!* I could head Hari's voice inside my head. I said,

'How are things?'

'Okay. How are they with you?'

'Not bad.'

'Have you got a new bike?'

'Yes. Present from my dad.'

'It's super.'

'I kind of think so. How's the viola playing?'

'Improving slowly.'

'Good.'

She smiled.

I coughed.

At that point I had to drag my bike into the gutter to avoid being mown down by a car which was coming up behind me and was cutting the bends fine. Glancing over my shoulder, I recognised the car. And the driver.

Viola waved to her father.

He drew up in front of us and wound down the window. 'Will you be long, dear? We're going to Aunt Mollie's for dinner, don't forget.'

'I'll be along in a minute.'

He gave me a short nod as if to say, I see you there. Would I want to go out with a girl who had a father like that? He drove off.

'I suppose I'd better be going,' said Viola.

I nodded. I didn't look at her.

'Sebastian, how would you like to go to the cinema some evening?'

Now I did look at her.

'Well, why shouldn't I ask you out? You believe in women's lib, don't you?'

'Yes, yes, of course,' I stuttered.

'So, what do you say?'

'Yes!'

I dropped the bike and grabbed her by the shoulders. She laughed and so did I and she said she had thought I would never ask her out and I said I had thought I never would either and we both laughed together.

'Tomorrow?' I said. 'Pick you up at seven?' I didn't care about her parents now. If they didn't like me they would just have to lump me! (As my grandmother would say.)

'See you!'

We parted and I went whizzing home, calling in on the way to tell Hari, who said, 'Thank goodness! At last! I was beginning to despair of you, boy.'

I couldn't keep the grin off my face as I walked into our flat.

'Uh-huh!' said Sam, guessing at once.

Torquil was present, though no longer seated in the best chair which had been reclaimed by our grandmother. Bella was wearing her new dress. There was an air of expectancy in the room.

'We have something to tell you,' said our mother.

Oh no! Surely Torquil wasn't going to move back in. I am kind of fond of him, in spite of a lot of things — well, he *is* my father — but the idea of having him living with us full-time would take a bit of getting used to. And we had hardly enough room as it was. And also, what would happen when the money ran out?

'Torquil and I are going off for a little holiday,' announced Bella.

'It won't be so little,' said Torquil. 'We're going away for two or three months, maybe longer, for as long as the money holds out.'

'We're going to wander round the Greek islands.'

Bella was now sounding dreamy. 'We can live quite inexpensively. Fruit and fish and cheap wine.'

'Two or three *months*?' I said. 'And what about us?'

'Well,' said Bella, the dreaminess gone. She turned her attention to our grandmother. 'Mother, I was thinking that perhaps you—'

'I what?'

'Might move in with the children while we're gone.'

'We could look after ourselves,' said Sam. 'And we could always go along for Granny if we needed her.'

'You're far too young to stay alone.'

'And what's to happen to the shop?' demanded Granny.

'I was thinking that perhaps you— Well, perhaps you could run the shop, with Sam's help on a Saturday. And Seb can do the books. I mean, now that you've no longer got your job—'

'Why shouldn't I enjoy my retirement? Don't you think I've done enough work in my life?'

'You said not so long ago that you weren't ready yet for the scrap heap.'

Our grandmother humphed and folded her arms under her bosom. Sam and I gazed at one another. We knew there would be no chance of us staying alone, no matter how much we went on. Bella may be an irresponsible parent, but she is not that irresponsible. Unfortunately.

And we knew, too, that Bella would come back. We weren't worried that she would go off and leave us for ever. We know her — and them — too well. They would go off on this second honeymoon feeling all romantic, but once they returned to Edinburgh life would resume as before. They can't live together but neither of them seems to be able to break the attachment that still joins them. Bella said this to me herself when we were sitting by the fire late one night.

We would miss her, though, and life with our grandmother would not be all a bed of roses. (As she herself might say.) But Bella might miss us, too, and even come back early. The thought cheered me. I doubted if they would last together for two months.

We waited. Granny would not be hurried. Eventually, she said, 'It seems like I've no choice, doesn't it? I know my duty, even if you do not at times, Isabel.'

'That's not fair, Mother!'

They were all set for an argy-bargy but Torquil intervened, saying, 'That's fantastic of you, Mother-in-law! I always knew you were a good sport.'

'Why can't *we* go to a Greek island?' asked Sam mournfully. 'I've never been abroad and Morag's been three times to Spain, once to Corfu, and once to Yugoslavia, and they're going to the Algarve for the half-term week.'

'You promised you'd take us to Greece sometime, Bella,' I said.

'You can come out and join us for half-term,' said Torquil. 'Well, I don't see why not?' He looked at Bella.

'Neither do I! It would be great fun. We'll buy the tickets for you before we go and we'll meet you in Athens.'

'Fantastic!' cried Sam, leaping up to half-strangle her with a hug. She then dropped a kiss on the top of Torquil's head and he smiled. I was feeling pretty pleased, too.

'Does that include me?' asked Granny.

Torquil's eyes boggled for a moment, then he rallied and said, 'Of course, Mother-in-law! We couldn't have a family party without you.'

130

'No show without Punch,' said Sam softly. (It's one of Granny's own sayings.) But Sam hadn't spoken softly enough. Granny rounded on her.

'I heard that, madam!'

'Sorry, Gran,' said Sam, as if butter wouldn't melt in her mouth.

Our grandmother did another humph. 'It's just as well I got early retirement if you ask me! It's a full-time job keeping this family on the rails.'

'And do you think you're succeeding, Gran?' I couldn't resist asking.

She looked the four of us over, like a colonel inspecting her troops. We pulled ourselves up out of our slouches but, even so, she didn't look too thrilled with what she saw.

'Never say die! — that's what I always say,' she said.

THE BURNING QUESTIONS OF BINGO BROWN
Betsy Byars

Has there ever been a successful writer named Bingo? Has there ever been a successful person with freckles? These are just some of the burning questions in Bingo Brown's life — but where is he going to find the answers? When his worst enemy moves in next door and Bingo keeps falling in love, he knows the question marks are getting larger. But with The Most Thrilling Day and The Worst News of his life still to come, Bingo finds he has a long way to go!

PRINCESS FLORIZELLA
Philippa Gregory

Poor Princess Florizella! She really isn't like other princesses at all. She isn't beautiful. She wants to share her palace with people who don't have homes. She loves eating huge meals, and she refuses to be rescued by a handsome prince, and never wants to marry anyone. But unfortunately her parents, a very ordinary King and Queen, have other ideas in mind.

MAGGIE AND ME
Ted Staunton

Maggie is the undisputed Greenapple Street Genius. She's always got some brilliant plan — and Cyril inevitably has to help her. Whether it's getting back at the school bully or swapping places for piano lessons, these best friends are forever having adventures. Poor Cyril! Life without Maggie would be an awful lot easier, but then it would be much more boring. What would he do if she ever moved away? Ten stories about the intrepid duo.

ROSCOE'S LEAP

Gillian Cross

To Hannah, living in a weird and fantastical old house means endlessly having to fix things like heating systems and furnaces, but for Stephen it is a place where something once happened to him, something dark and terrifying which he doesn't want to remember but cannot quite forget. Then a stranger intrudes upon the family and asks questions about the past that force Hannah to turn her attention from mechanical things to human feelings, and drive Stephen to meet the terror that is locked away inside him, waiting . . .

OVER THE MOON AND FAR AWAY

Margaret Nash

The new girl at school calls herself a 'traveller' and says she comes from beyond the stars. Ben doesn't believe her, of course, but then again Zillah isn't quite like anyone he and his friends have ever met. There's her name for a start, and she doesn't even know how to play their games. But the mysterious newcomer does seem able to make things happen . . .

THE TROUBLE WITH JACOB

Eloise McGraw

Right from the start there is something very weird about the boy Andy sees on the hillside. Every time Andy's twin sister Kat is there he just disappears, and all he ever talks about is his bed! Andy thinks he's going mad, but then he and Kat decide that someone is playing tricks on them. There must be some logical solution to the mystery. After all, the only other explanation would be far too incredible . . .